Her Co

Rodeo bronc supplier Lori Calhoun has struggled to live up to expectations after her father's sudden death. When a trailer load of her star broncs disappears, the Knight Agency steps in to investigate.

Foreman of the Calhoun Ranch, Trip Jensen has watched Lori struggle to keep up with the demands of the ranch and the rodeo stock. He's always admired her and loved her—but he's kept that to himself. She was the boss's daughter and is now the boss…off-limits for a cowboy like him. When more stock begins to disappear from the ranch, they must work together to solve the mystery. Unable to know who on the ranch to trust Trip enlist the Presley brothers from the neighboring ranch to back him up.

Lori has always admired Trip but he made it clear years ago that he wasn't interested in her as more than a friend. Now, he sticking close and she's finding it hard to concentrate on the danger and not the man.

Can love blossom between them before time runs out?

HER COWBOY HERO

Cowboys of Ransom Creek, Book One

DEBRA CLOPTON

Her Cowboy Hero

Copyright © 2017 Debra Clopton Parks

CHAPTER ONE

“The horses and the trailer are gone.”

What? Lori Calhoun stared at Trip Jensen, her foreman at the Calhoun Ranch and also her partner in the rough stock rodeo contracting business—thanks to her father.

The pit of her stomach knotted as she saw the solemn look in Trip's eyes.

“All five of them?” she asked, fighting the shock of finding out their prized saddle broncs had been stolen.

Trip shifted his weight from one boot to the other.

His handsome features twisted with disgust and fury as he squinted at her from beneath the straw Stetson shading his light-blue eyes. "Yep. They're gone. But we will find them. Harvey and Mike said they loaded the horses on the trailer before they connected it to the truck. Don't ask me why they did that. Then they went to get the truck—which was, for some reason, still on the other side of the arena. When they got back, the trailer loaded with our horses had disappeared."

She blinked through frustrations strangling her. "That doesn't even sound right. What was Harvey thinking?"

"I don't know," Trip bit out, showing his frustration. "I have no reason to believe that he or Mike had anything to do with the theft—other than lack of good judgment—but believe me, I'm looking into it."

Her stomach churned. Those were her champion rodeo broncs and the mainstay of the rough stock business. Those horses were headed to the Western Rodeo Circuit finals if they kept performing like they had this year. They were the cornerstone of the business, but she didn't need to tell Trip that. Like her, he had a stake in this business and understood all too well how important it was for their horses to be in the finals this year.

So much had happened this year. Her father had died in a tragic horse accident—that alone still held her in the grips of grief. But on top of that, everyone would be watching to see whether she and Trip could continue with the tradition of Calhoun stock in the WRC finals that had begun the first year her daddy had formed the stock contracting business. Trip had bought half the company only three months before Ray Calhoun's horse threw him. He hit his head and died, and left her to take the reins of the ranch and the other half of the stock company. And Lori was struggling.

Add to that her mounting frustration at being forced, by her dad, to work with Trip.

Those frustrations had been mounting for the last five months, threatening to explode, and now this... She swung around to stare out the window. Fighting anger and insecurities, she slammed her fist to her hips and studied the barns and arenas across the wide yard and gravel parking area. This was the ranch her daddy had built. The ranch that now rested on her shoulders and she felt in every way that she was not living up to expectations.

"Daddy would be furious right now," she said.

He'd been dead only five months and she felt as if she was in over her head. He would be rolling over in his grave right now if he knew that on her watch she'd lost such a legacy.

"It's not your fault, Lori. It's not mine either. Someone did this and we're going to find out who. It's that simple. Your dad wouldn't be mad at you. Them—yes. No doubt about that."

She spun back to glare at Trip. "This happened on my watch—and so did that trailer load of steers that someone just drove off the property last week."

"Lori Lyn Calhoun, I'm warning you to stop blaming yourself. You didn't lose those broncs or that load of heifers. It's only a matter of time before we catch them. Those rangers will get a lead on them. As for the load of horses, Harvey and Mike lost them on *my* watch. And I plan to find them."

"Our watch," she snapped, stubbornly. "Do you think Harvey and Mike are guilty?"

"Of carelessness. But until I get better answers as to why they loaded that trailer and then left it unattended with our prized stock in it, I'm not going to be easy to live with. And they won't be careless like that again."

She took a deep breath and tried to hold onto her show of strength. But the façade was growing thin. Since her dad's death, she felt so alone. Her mother had turned her back on her when she was a baby and it had just been her and her dad. And then, there was Trip...she pushed away the overpowering wish to feel his strong arms around her. Once, things had been so easy between them. Once, that would have been an option.

But it hadn't been for a very long time. "So, what do we do now?" she asked instead, gaining strength from him.

"I've called the cops and reported it. I've also called the Knight Agency—since they know the rodeo and investigate incidents for the WRC, they may be able to find out more than the police. They basically asked Harvey and Mike a couple of questions, then told them they'd be in touch if they hear anything. Since this was a WRC-sanctioned rodeo, the Knights have taken the lead."

"That's good to know."

"I think they'll get to the bottom of it."

She bit her lip. "This will be a first that the Calhoun Ranch or the stock company has ever been in the middle of a rodeo investigation."

She didn't think that was a fluke. No, her dad, Ray Calhoun, had been one tough cowboy. He'd built this ranch and the rough stock business from the ground up and he was as tough as the bucking horses they bred. Her daddy was a hard businessman, a hard rider, and a harder man when it came to being crossed.

"There's a first for everything," Trip said. "But that doesn't mean we have to like it or take it."

"Right," she grunted. "I'm pretty certain nobody messed with Daddy simply because of who he was." But she wasn't her daddy. She was just his daughter, trying hard to step into his boots and knowing no one could ever replace him. She fought off the sudden need to cry and wished she still had her back to Trip.

"You're doing a good job, Lori." He took a step toward her, but stopped. "Your dad would be proud of you for sticking around and stepping in for him."

For a brief moment, it felt like it once had, when things were easy between them...before everything had gotten so complicated.

She sighed. "I'm trying. But this isn't helping." She wanted desperately to live up to the expectation of her dad...her daddy. He deserved only the best she could give because that was what he'd always given to her.

When Lori was two, her mother ran off with another man and hadn't wanted anything to do with Lori or her dad. He had tried to love Lori enough for himself and her runaway mother, and that meant he'd spoiled her in many ways. But he'd raised her to be independent, too. And when eventually she'd chosen to take a job in Houston instead of staying here and running the ranch with him, he'd given her his blessing. She'd been in Houston when she'd gotten the call that he was dead.

Devastated was too small a word for what she'd felt. What she still felt.

She still carried the wound that she'd not been here on the ranch where she belonged when he'd had his accident. She didn't think she would ever get over that.

And now this.

She focused on Trip, standing solid and strong as he waited for her to speak. For only a moment, she wished again that she could rest her head on his shoulder and feel the support of his arms around her. She pushed that thought out of her mind. This was not the time for regrets or a show of weakness. Instead, she pushed her shoulders back and yanked her big-girl pants up. She was Ray Calhoun's daughter. "What did the Knights say? Fill me in and let's get on this. I do not plan to stand by and let vultures start pecking off bits and pieces of my daddy's legacy."

Trip smiled. "Well, hello Lori Calhoun. Where the dickens have you been lately?"

Her heart clenched. "Having a pity party. And I

just realized my daddy raised me better than that."

She thought she saw approval in Trip's gaze. "The police said they'll call if they hear anything. They're on the lookout for the trailer, though I'm not holding out any hope, since whoever did this probably changed the plates. If not, then I figure the trailer is abandoned somewhere empty. As for the Knights, Sean Knight was at the rodeo in case a veterinarian was needed, since that's his job. He'd already left the grounds, but is hanging around the area and not flying home since the next WRC rodeo is at the Fort Worth Stockyards next week. So he's supposed to meet me at the arena in Mesquite at three."

"Great. I'll join you, then." She glanced at her watch. "When are we leaving?"

"It's a two-hour drive from Ransom Creek to the arena, so how about right after lunch?"

"Perfect. I'll meet you at the truck at one."

"Sounds good. I better go to my office and get a few things done." Then, without another word, he headed out the door of her daddy's office. Her office.

Unable to stop herself, she moved to the window

and watched him move with purposeful strides across the yard toward the stables that also housed the ranch manager's office—his office.

Nearly a decade-old longing seeped over her. Their relationship was complicated. And she'd learned to live with things the way they were years ago, after he'd headed off to college and left her behind. Thought she might one day get over him...

And then her daddy had hired him on as manager and gone into business with him.

Then he'd complicated things more by dying and leaving her here to sort things out.

Complicated.

Her life in a nutshell.

It took everything Trip had in him to walk out of that house without pulling Lori into his arms and trying to comfort her. She was being too hard on herself, having lost her dad and then stepping into the ownership of the ranch and the rodeo stock company. She had a lot on her shoulders, and trying to live up to the expectations of her father, or others' expectations, was not making things any easier. And then dealing with him as ranch manager...things had been strained between them ever since she'd come home from Houston to deal with the ranch's needs after Ray's death.

She had a life in Houston and he wasn't certain whether she planned to go back to that life when things were sorted out here, or whether she planned to stay.

One thing he knew: his time was running out to bridge this canyon between them. And the horses being stolen wasn't helping anything. It was just adding more burden on her already loaded-down shoulders.

He hurt for her. It was hard knowing his being here added more strain on her. It was hard on him, too. But he was determined to make things right between them.

CHAPTER TWO

Sean Knight showed up at the Mesquite arena on time. Lori and Trip had made the two-hour drive and arrived just before him.

Despite all that they had going on, she found that, inside the truck, the awkwardness that had been between them since she'd taken over the ranch intensified. The close quarters seemed to draw in on her and she was so aware of him as a man that it was nearly overwhelming.

She'd managed to keep up a stilted conversation about ranch business and how best to cope with the loss of the missing horses. The man smelled entirely too good and it was all she could do not to sigh or inhale in desperate gulps. Unrequited love was the pits. Pure and simple, it was torture. She'd kept her end of the conversation flowing, but no matter how hard she tried, their unfinished business from high school hung in the air between them like an elephant clinging to a tightrope.

They'd been the best of friends growing up, then they'd matured. The fact that she'd wanted more than friendship from him—aka, a life with him—and he hadn't wanted the same thing had been hard to get over. But she had.

And then her dad had thrown them together again by hiring Trip and then dying. She was mad at him for both.

When they reached the Mesquite rodeo arena, she almost threw herself out of the truck in her desperation to get out. She'd never been so thankful to be out of the close confines of the truck in all of her life. Trip smelled too good, his voice sounded too good—and none of that kind of thinking was good for her.

No, those kinds of thoughts would do nothing but cause her misery, and right now, with her dad's loss, she had enough of that to deal with.

Sean Knight was waiting for them. He held out his hand; he and Trip shook and then his sympathetic gaze touched her. "We were all sorry to hear about your dad. He was a good man."

"Thank you. It's still so hard to believe, but I'm doing okay. I was blessed to have him in my life. But you know how that is. My dad always liked your dad. He would be so proud of all of you."

"Thanks. Now let's take a look around. These horses disappearing like this from the rodeo is pretty bold."

"Tell me about it," Trip agreed. "Who would just hook up to someone else's trailer and drive off? I guess it being dark helped."

"Probably so. And it was busy, so maybe no one would have paid attention, but then again, maybe someone did. We'll see what we can dig up by asking around. Can you tell me what you know?"

Trip filled him in about Harvey and Mike and

everything they knew so far. She followed them to the spot where the trailer had last been sitting. The area was dirt with various tracks all around, including the markings from where their trailer had been parked. But everywhere there were very near identical markings from where all the other trailers from the rodeo had set. It looked impossible.

"I don't see how looking around here is going to help find my...our horses." She amended the statement with a glance at Trip. She was still adjusting her thought process to their being partners on the rough stock.

Both men glanced up from where they were studying the ground and she suddenly hated that she had voiced her negative thoughts. But there were so many tracks and boots in this area.

She kept her gaze off Trip and focused on Sean.

He gave her a reassuring smile. "I get where you're coming from, Lori. But we need to start here. It just happened last night, and it was nice that we had a short drizzle during the day yesterday so that we have all these tracks today. These tire tracks here aren't from your truck, since it wasn't hooked up to the trailer. So these have to be from the truck that took your horses. That's a good thing. And despite all this foot traffic, all these boot prints are good." He moved to a cluster of boot tracks. "This is where the trailer hitch was. Whoever stood here was hooking the truck and trailer. It's a jumble, but we might be able to get something usable from them." He pulled his phone out and snapped pictures.

Trip went to stand beside Sean and she was left feeling like a negative ninny.

"There were at least two different men standing here," Trip said.

"Exactly," Sean agreed. "They could be the thieves. That is a distinctive marking of the boot heel. Notice how the back of the heel is heavily worn on the outer edge."

She moved to look. "Oh, I see what you're saying."

For the first time since Trip had told her the news that her top-ranked horses were stolen, she felt a glimmer of hope. "I'm sorry about being negative."

Sean looked sympathetic. "I get it. Cimarron Trouble is one of the best broncs on the circuit, and the other four are right up there too. This has to be an upsetting situation for you. The WRC has had its fair share of bad luck this season, but we'll help out any way we can to get your horses back."

Her gaze shifted to Trip. He gave her a small smile, his lip curving upward on one side and causing an unwanted flutter in her chest.

"We're going to find them," he assured her. He turned away, leaving her staring at his strong back as he scanned the ground.

She watched him, and then her gaze collided with Sean's. No doubt he could feel the tension between them; it hung in the area despite Trip's tight smile.

"What should I look for?" she asked Sean, feeling self-conscious.

"Anything that seems worthwhile." He went back to looking around himself.

"How about this cigarette butt?" Trip asked from where he stood several feet away. "I know there are a lot of cowboys who smoke, but I can't place any of my men who do. Maybe this will come in handy."

Sean went to look. "Maybe so. It's not faded at all, so it looks recent."

Sean pulled a plastic baggie from his pocket. He also pulled a pair of tweezers from a small pouch he was carrying. "Good call." He picked the butt up with the tweezers, placed it in the bag, and sealed it up.

Deciding the best thing she could do was to look around herself, Lori got busy, determined to contribute rather than complain. She studied the indentation where the trailer had been. There were several footprints along the side of the trailer tires. "Maybe these belong to someone involved?"

Sean agreed. "Could be. We'll want to look at your men's boots and see if the imprints match."

"That can be arranged," Trip said.

"Until we know whether or not one of your men has these imprints, we won't know if this is a significant break or not."

She tried to remember whether one of her guys walked with a sway or leaned heavily on one leg. Anything that might mean an imprint with an awkward back heel like the print Sean had found near the hitch area. Harvey had a little weight on him, but Mike was skinny as a fence post. But like Trip had said earlier, they had no reason to suspect either man of anything but carelessness.

Sean knelt down and rested his elbows on his knees, his cotton shirt stretched tight across his shoulders as he studied them. "It looks like three separate imprints. Different from the first one at the trailer hitch. There should be two imprints at the trailer hitch—one of them will be your man and one set could be the horse thief's."

Sean took several more photos and Trip took some as well. "See the depth of this imprint? It's deeper than the other two, which probably means he's heavier, so my guess would be that we are dealing with two of a similar weight and one heavier."

Trip frowned. "Harvey's not the smallest guy. He's about six feet and over two hundred pounds, I would estimate. Mike is smaller, about five-nine but less than a hundred and seventy."

"We'll want their imprints," Sean said.

She looked at Trip. Unease turned in her stomach. "You don't think Harvey's involved, do you? Daddy hired him several years ago. I really can't imagine him being involved in this."

"Then there's nothing for him to worry about," Sean said. "We aren't accusing him of anything. But I still need to compare his boot imprint with that one. I'm not claiming or insinuating guilt of any sort. I just need a process of elimination to figure out who these prints belong to so that we can decide if these are clues. They can help us along the way."

She nodded, getting what he was saying, and tried not to feel guilty about not trusting the men who worked for her.

"Trip tells me you had dealings with rustlers a week ago?"

"Yes. So far nothing has turned up."

"Okay, I'll relay that back to my brothers when we look at all the factors."

They spent the next few minutes discussing what the agency could do and if they could help at all. "We'll just have to see," Sean said. "Until we dig deeper, we really don't know what we're dealing with. I'll head out to your ranch in the morning and do a few interviews. I'll just tell them I'm following up where the police left off. At this point, we aren't accusing anyone of anything. Maybe someone noticed something the police missed in their questioning. After that, I'll drive back to Dallas and catch my plane."

Lori nodded and met Trip's gaze. His brow hitched slightly, as if questioning whether she was okay with this. She wasn't okay with any of it. "That's fine. We'll be ready for you."

She just hoped that questioning her men didn't cause them to believe she didn't trust them. She already struggled to have them give her half the respect they'd given her father. She certainly didn't need to alienate them.

They were quiet as they left the arena and headed back toward the ranch. She raked a hand through her hair. Her thoughts swirled.

"I'll make sure all the men stay near the main compound in the morning so we can talk to them," Trip said. "It'll be good to see if anyone saw anything or heard anything out of the ordinary over the last few months. I'm not sure exactly what we're looking for, but maybe slinging questions out is the way to uncover something. I know you're worried how the men will take this, but stop worrying. It's your ranch, Lori. You have a right to answers and to ask anything you want to know. And as far as these horses go, so do I."

True, she told herself. "Still, I just took over the ranch, and this isn't going to endear me to the men. I'm already the daughter of the boss."

"And for the ones who can't handle that, I'll show them the door."

They'd been over this again and again. He'd fired three guys not long after she'd taken over for that very thing. They'd just not liked the fact that a twenty-seven-year-old woman was their boss.

"No, I don't want to do that again. No one has been rude like those others were. And I can't help feeling like I shouldn't have let them go."

She felt him tense. They'd been at odds over this from the beginning, too. Silence held the inside of the truck captive.

"You're my boss, but you know I disagree with you on that."

And that was part of their problem...she hated being Trip Jensen's boss. Yes, they were partners in the stock contracting company, but as for the ranch, she was his boss and he didn't seem to be able to forget that.

In the few months that her dad had been alive after he'd hired Trip, she'd been able to ignore how awkward this was going to be because she was almost two hundred miles away from the ranch, living in Houston. But then her dad died, and she'd taken a leave of absence and come home to sort things out. And being Trip's boss along with everything else in their past was not helping the tough situation she faced of picking up the pieces.

Trip's grip on the steering wheel tightened as regrets pounded him like baseball-sized hail. He fought hard not to overstep his boundaries, reminding himself that he was only the foreman, the manager. He was not

Lori's keeper. As much as he wanted to be more to her, he wasn't. And he had to keep reminding himself of that fact. It got harder with every passing day they worked together.

"Do you really think that they'll find anything?"

"They have a great reputation, so they're the best shot and that's why I called them."

"That was a good call. I hope we get this figured out soon." She grew quiet and nodded, then went back to watching the pastures go by.

He glanced at her profile. She looked tense. Before he could let the boss/employee relationship stop him, he reached out and took her hand. "It's going to be all right," he assured her.

She met his gaze with wide sea-blue eyes, and for a moment she looked so vulnerable. She was no longer the girl who'd befriended him that first day his dad had taken him to the ranch after being hired as the foreman. Trip had been ten, and she was nine. Now, in that split second, he felt transported to old times. When she had trusted him. It had been so long since there had been an easiness between them.

"I hope so." She removed her hand from his.

A band tightened around his heart. He'd been a lonesome kid when they'd moved to Ransom Creek for the new job and moved into the manager's house on the ranch. Lori had been a skinny, freckled-faced girl with pigtails, and that first day she'd been wearing a pink shirt with blue jeans tucked into pink boots. Lori Calhoun had been one sassy little girl. He almost smiled remembering how she'd marched over to him as he got out of the truck.

"You know how to ride?" she'd asked, looking at him skeptically.

He'd been highly offended. "Of course I can ride," he'd boasted, and she'd grinned wide, exposing a missing tooth.

"Not as good as me," she'd said. "Come on, let's saddle up."

And from that day forward, they were friends. And she'd been right, that scrawny girl could ride a horse better than most grown men. Her daddy had taught her well.

They'd grown up together on the ranch and been

the best of friends as kids. They'd ridden every inch of the ranch together, climbed the hills and followed the trails, herding cattle and chasing strays. That had been when life was simple.

When she was about sixteen and he was just about to turn seventeen, he knew she was the girl for him. And that was when things got complicated.

His dad had taken him aside and pointed out the facts of life as far as their family was concerned—Lori was the boss's daughter and Trip was the manager's son. She would always own the ranch and he worked the ranch. And that was an impasse that he didn't need to cross. His dad also pointed out that if Trip dated Lori and they broke up, it could put his management job in jeopardy.

A weight had settled on Trip's shoulders and on his heart at that moment. And it had changed the course of his and Lori's relationship. He'd backed away his senior year, knowing he had to. He had nothing to offer her. Nothing. And so he'd graduated and taken a job on a ranch near Texas A&M, and worked hard to help put himself through college. Then he went to work right out of college, selling a top brand feed, and hit the road. He saved every penny he could, socking it away for his future.

He hadn't loved his job, but the pay was good and the commissions even better. He'd dated some, but Lori had stayed in his heart. He'd tried not to care when he got word she was in a serious relationship in Houston. Tried not to care when he'd heard her relationship had fallen through. And he'd tried not to care the day her daddy had called him and offered him the ranch manager job after Trip's own daddy had announced he was retiring.

Trip had refused the offer to come back and take over where his dad left off. The pay had been great, the opportunity undeniable—if a man wanted to manage someone else's ranch. None of that would help Trip own his own ranch or win the woman of his dreams.

When Lori's dad had called back, being open about wanting to ensure the ranch was in good shape for Lori if something were to happen to him, Trip had understood where Ray was coming from. But being foreman still left him in the same position he'd always been in where Lori was concerned. As if he understood Trip's dilemma, Ray had counter-offered with the manager's job, plus the opportunity to buy in as half-owner of the rough stock contracting company.

Trip had taken the deal.

He'd sunk his savings into the offer and now his future rode on the success of the rough stock business. If he could help grow the business and build it, then he could let his feelings for Lori be known.

It was getting tougher to keep them hidden with every day he was here.

He needed to know where they stood and he needed to get past the barrier of polite professionalism that was wedged between them.

CHAPTER THREE

The next day, Sean showed up to the ranch, and he went about interviewing the two men who had lost his trailer. Just like Lori feared, Harvey took offense at being questioned by Sean.

"I already answered the police's questions. Now you've hired a private eye to investigate me? Your daddy always trusted me."

She started to say something but Trip beat her to it.

"Harvey, we're not accusing you of anything but carelessness, which you and I both know Ray would not have stood for, so stop with the guilt trip and answer Sean's questions. We're just looking for leads."

The two men stared at each other and Lori knew what Trip had said about her daddy was true.

"Fine," Harvey grunted and then glared at Sean.

Sean had remained neutral in the conflict, as if he was used to this sort of thing. Lori wasn't. But she had to admit now that Harvey had been so disagreeable she was determined that he would answer the questions, even if she was the one who ended up asking them.

Sean looked at Harvey's boots. It was logical that one set of prints near the hitch would be his. It wasn't the pair with the uneven heel. Harvey's had a little normal wear but he didn't have an exaggerated worn edge like the one at the scene.

After an irritated but somewhat cooperative Harvey left, they called in Mike. He also had a worn-down boot heel.

"Did you see anything that might get your suspicions up?" Sean asked him.

"I'm afraid not. There was nobody around while I was there—it was just me. We loaded the horses, and I locked the trailer up. Then we went and got in the truck. I didn't think anything about leaving the horses there. Most everyone was packing up and heading out. We see the same people at every rodeo. It never occurred to us someone would do this."

Mike had only been working on the ranch for four months. Trip had hired him right after he'd fired the three who hadn't liked the idea of a female boss.

Sean looked at the two of them when he'd finished the interviews. They'd found a couple of their ranch hands who had a boot heel that could possibly be a match to the one near the trailer hitch.

"So far, all we have is several cowboys with slanted boot heels," Sean said.

"And there are a lot of bowlegged cowboys out there with slanted boot heels." Lori sighed.

"But still, we have a cigarette butt and a slanted boot heel, and when we get a break, one of those could be the ace in our pocket," Sean added. "I've got to head out if I'm going to catch my flight. We'll see you in Fort Worth. Call if you have more information. I'll do some digging and some background checks on the men working here if you'll send me the list of names. Something about all of this still doesn't feel right."

"I can do that," Trip said as they stood and headed out of the office.

Sean looked around. "So you own the ranch," he said to Lori. "And you both own the stock contracting business? I'm not convinced this is WRC related. Those cattle being stolen could be connected to your horses being stolen."

"Yes," Lori said. "We've been thinking that too."

They stopped at Sean's truck. "So, my advice is to be on your watch. I hate to say it, but don't trust anyone."

Trip met her gaze.

Did Sean mean each other?

Sean's truck disappeared in a cloud of dust, but his words hung in the air around Trip and Lori. He turned to her. "Do you trust me?"

She squinted at him in the sunlight as she pushed her dark hair behind her ear. "We might have our differences, but the truth is that Sean could have told me straight up that you were stealing from me and I wouldn't have believed him. He was talking about everyone else working for us."

Relief washed through Trip and he fought down the need to smile. Instead, he met her serious gaze with a nod. "Okay then, that means a lot."

"So where do we go from here?" she asked, holding his gaze.

Her words brought up a whole host of wishful thinking on his part. "Want to take a walk and look at the stock heading to Fort Worth?" He needed to move.

"Sure." She fell into step with him as he started to walk.

"We need to do whatever it takes to figure this out," he said. "And I think you should know that while I don't like the idea of this being an inside job like Sean implied, I'm not discounting it. Your daddy hired me because he knew he could trust me with all the things he cared about." They reached the holding pen, and he looked at her. "We came to an understanding because we had a common goal." Trip's heart was galloping as he said the words. He and Lori's dad had always had the same goal when it came to Lori. She meant the world to both of them.

At Trip's words and the look in his pale-blue eyes, a shiver of awareness raced through Lori. His gaze rested on her lips and then lifted to meet her eyes. "Are you talking about me?"

"What else would I be talking about, Lori?" he asked, his voice roughening.

Her skin tingled, and she swallowed hard. Suddenly she needed to change the subject. It was getting too close to something she didn't want to acknowledge, something she was scared to acknowledge for fear once again her hopes and dreams would be dashed and her heart broken.

She moved a step away from him. It was either that or else she feared she'd throw herself at him, and that would not do.

"Do you think my daddy had something wrong with him? I just—I just can't come to grips with the fact that he was thrown from his horse." She hadn't voiced that concern to anyone.

Trip was quiet. She wasn't sure whether it was because she'd changed the subject or because her question had startled him.

"No," he said finally. "He didn't say anything. And if he was having issues, I never noticed it. Sometimes things just happen. Flukes, oddities," he said, his voice gentle. "If a horse trips anyone, even the best horseman in the business can have an accident."

Lori nodded and felt moisture at the corner of her eyes. She blinked hard. *She would not cry.* She took a shaky breath. He'd stood beside her at the funeral, as her ranch manager, and she'd longed for her friend...

But she'd lost him when she'd pushed for their relationship to be more during the end of her junior year. He'd pulled away almost instantly and distanced himself, and then left for college and broke her heart.

Now, despite fighting her feelings for him and all the conflicting emotions she was facing right now, she would settle for just having her friend back.

But it wasn't that simple.

Anger spiked through her suddenly. She'd had her daddy's death to deal with, a ranch to sort out, and in all of that, she was being forced to fight these unwanted emotions over Trip.

Her horses going missing was not helping. She'd let her defenses down because, until now, they'd been strictly business.

"You're right. I just can't imagine him being thrown from a horse." She took a step back from Trip. "I need to call the insurance company about filing a claim on the horses." She stepped back another step and fought for calm.

He looked conflicted but just nodded curtly in agreement. She fought the desire to throw herself into his arms and cry on his chest. Instead, she spun and hurried toward the house...trying hard not to run.

Trip held himself stiffly where he stood and watched her hurry toward the ranch house. He rubbed the back of his neck and wondered at the wisdom of taking this job. But then, he understood why Ray had wanted him here, why he'd even been willing to sell half the stock contracting business to Trip. He wanted Lori safe and so did Trip. But Lori...he was beginning to wonder whether he'd made the wrong decision for Lori.

Was their decision fair to Lori?

For a brief moment, it had felt like old times, when they'd been friends and confided everything to each other. And then she'd back-stepped.

Torn with what to do, he headed toward his truck. He had a bull to look at and he needed to put a little distance between him and Lori for a little while.

She'd probably thank him.

CHAPTER FOUR

Joleen DeLeon stared at Lori in the mirror of the Fluff-n-Buff Hair Salon two days after the horses went missing. "Girl, it has been far too long since you had these nasty split ends snipped off," she drawled, and then leaned in so no one else in the salon could hear. "So how's it going with your hunky foreman? Have you let bygones be bygones and opened a new chapter in your love life?"

"Joleen, I have a lot going on at the ranch. I have cattle missing and now horses missing."

Her old friend shrugged. "So, more excuses to

cuddle up with Trip-you-are-so-fine-Jensen." She pointed her comb at Lori and her eyes narrowed. "Do not tell me you are still holding that grudge. You and that man were this close growing up." She locked two fingers together and waggled them at Lori. "Y'all were kids. You've both been out in the world and come back home to roost and you're both still single. Let it go and see where it goes."

Lori glared at Joleen. "Has it ever occurred to you that I may not have been in to get a trim because of the harassment you gave me about Trip last time?"

"Has it ever occurred to you that I could cut six inches off your hair in one swipe if you keep denying you still have feelings for that man? I think your daddy, God rest his hardheaded soul, knew it too. And this is his way of making the pathway clear."

"Could we change the subject, please? And are you going to trim or just harass me?"

Joleen gave a coy smile. "I'll trim but I really enjoy harassing you. You get so uptight. That's how I know you still care, despite all your protesting. You do know that ever since he moved back, he's been a hot topic with the gals. But he has yet to ask any one of them out—though plenty of them have practically thrown themselves in front of his truck in an attempt to get his attention."

Try as she might, jealousy rose inside Lori at the thought of other women trying to win a date with Trip. "That doesn't mean anything to me except that he's busy at the ranch since Daddy died and he has too much on his mind to notice them."

"It could mean he has you on his mind. I remember the way he used to look at you in school. He practically adored you and it was not in a my-best-friend kind of way. That hot high school hunk was crazy about you, and even after you two had your blowup, I'd catch him watching you from a distance. And believe me, girlfriend, he looked like one lovesick cowboy, the same longing look he'd always had for you. It never made sense to me that you two split instead of getting closer."

Lori fought down any feelings of hope her friend's words might cause. "I really need to get back to the ranch. Can you hurry?"

Joleen gave a shrug. "Okay. Relax. I'll back off. You look stressed and the last thing I want to do is add to that."

"Thanks. For everything."

With a new trim and an earful of gossip, Lori stopped by the grocery store and then headed back to the ranch. It had helped to get away. She'd been trying for two days to avoid Trip and it hadn't been hard, which meant he'd been letting her avoid him or trying just as hard to avoid her, which didn't sound like Trip.

With Joleen's voice echoing in her head, she headed home. Had Joleen really seen Trip staring at her with longing?

If that were so, then why had he pulled back when she'd practically thrown herself at him the week before her prom? Why had he spent the following year avoiding her like the plague?

She carried her groceries inside the house, put them away, and then stood at the window, staring out at the barn. *Was he there, in his office?* She'd run like a scared rabbit after their conversation at the round pens. There was just so much going on and too many emotions floating around.

She'd thought about him for the last two days. She had horses missing and bookings on the verge of canceling if they couldn't get the stock back, and what was on her mind? Trip and the way they'd once been.

Some ranch woman she was turning out to be.

Yes, she'd taken care of business, contacted the insurance company, answered all the police questions, and was gearing up to head to Fort Worth at the end of the week. And then Oklahoma City—if they didn't cancel on her. They had a heavy schedule, but now with her five best horses missing, they were in jeopardy of losing some of their contracts.

The one blessing in all of this was that the insurance claim could help with their financial loss. But she *wanted* her horses back.

She wanted a lot of things—Trip Jensen, for starters—and it was driving her crazy. She so wanted to end this rollercoaster of emotions that Trip had her on.

She needed to stop hiding out from him. With that on her mind, she walked to the barn. Maybe a ride would do her good. The men were sorting cattle today; maybe she'd ride out there and help. A ride sounded good, and it had been a long time since she'd cut calves from a herd.

As she entered the stable, Harvey almost ran over her as he stormed out of Trip's office. His face was red and the anger in his expression was vivid.

"Harvey, what's the matter?" she asked, startled by the fury in his expression.

He scowled. "Well, I guess I'll be telling you that I don't like people looking at me like I did something wrong." He glared at her and something inside her snapped.

She'd had enough. "No one has accused you of anything, but we had a right to ask questions." She met his stare straight on. "Sean simply asked you a few questions that you should have been willing and *ready* to answer. I don't understand why you're so upset, and quite frankly, I'm about fed up with it," she said, firmly feeling herself channeling her dad.

Harvey looked startled and suddenly at a loss for words.

She wasn't. "You were at the rodeo and you were responsible for those animals, and if you're going to continue to work here, then you need to own up to that fact. Those animals are a huge loss to this business. Answering a few questions when I'm out five prize rodeo stock is not too much to ask. You should have expected questions."

They stared at each other. Her temper wasn't usually so quick, but really, what was Harvey thinking? That they were just supposed to let her— *their*—animals disappear and not ask any questions? Behind him, she saw Trip come to the door of his office.

"I guess you're right," Harvey muttered.

"I know I'm right." She couldn't help it. Over Harvey's shoulder, she saw Trip press one shoulder to the doorframe as he relaxed against it, crossed his arms, and watched quietly. Supporting her but not intruding unless she needed him.

Her insides quivered. She focused on Harvey.

"Yes, ma'am," he grunted. "But I got a feeling that nobody trusts me around here. Even though I have been here all these years. Your daddy would've trusted me."

Guilt hit her, but she quickly dismissed it. "Yes, he would have. He hired you a long time ago, Harvey. But that doesn't mean he would have let you get by without answering some questions and you know it."

It hit her then that maybe Harvey might have thought he would move into the foreman position when Trip's dad had retired. Instead, her dad had brought in Trip.

Could he have been involved—no. She wasn't going to think that. She actually trusted Harvey, though she was disappointed in his response to this situation.

"This will pass, Harvey," she said. "But until it does, questions might be asked. We're just trying to get to the bottom of this."

Her words didn't make him look any happier. "Fine," he grunted and walked off.

She watched him go and then looked at Trip. He hitched an eyebrow and then backed into his office; she followed him inside and closed the door behind her.

"So what exactly did you say to Harvey that had him so upset?" she asked.

Trip leaned on the edge of his desk and crossed his arms as he studied her. "I just asked him if he remembered anything since being interviewed about the incident and why he loaded the horses before hooking the truck to the trailer. Nothing he should have gotten all huffed up about."

She sighed, letting her breath out slowly. "You're right. But he's been here for years. I can't believe he'd be a part of stealing them. I'm not ready to believe the worst, not until we have more facts. I just won't jump to conclusions. Harvey feels like we're accusing him of something and I'm—*we're* not. Still, we have to keep an open mind and someone did this. So I'm not trusting anybody except you and me."

"You're thinking what I'm thinking. And Harvey has no right to accuse us of anything."

She nodded, glad to have his support. It felt good knowing she had his backing. "I'm going to Fort Worth with you. I'm going to be on watch and have my ears open too."

"I think that's a good idea. It'll be nice to have you around."

She ran a hand through her hair. "I'm going for a ride. I need to get out in the open for a little while."

"You holding up okay?" he asked, his gaze penetrating.

She shrugged. "I'm doing the best I can. This on top of Daddy only being dead a few months…" She hesitated, considering her words. She'd been trying so hard to be strong.

"You want some company on your ride?"

Her pulse sped up. Once, the two of them had ridden everywhere on the ranch together. "Sure, just like old times," she said, trying to keep herself neutral. "But I don't want to talk about all this. I haven't slept much and I just want a break for a few minutes. I just want a ride. Can you do that?"

His lip hitched up on the side. "I can do that because I'm in total agreement with you that you need a break. And you need some sleep. Maybe if we ride, your mind will relax a bit. And I'd love to show you some of the changes we've done since you rode the ranch. Your dad was always making improvements. Of course, by truck you could see more, but there are a few things to see close enough for a ride."

"That's a great idea. We can give it our best shot, anyway." She took a deep breath. She had a sense of exhilaration at the thought of riding with him...*her old friend*, she reminded herself. It wasn't safe to think of him as anything else. He'd made it perfectly clear that they had a professional relationship these days.

His grin, though, made it a hard thing to remember. They headed into the stable. She picked a pretty mare she'd ridden in the arena a few times since she'd been home, and he grabbed his black gelding. They brushed them down and saddled them and then headed out toward the horizon. The simple act of leaving the house and ranch compound behind her gave a sense of relief from her shoulders. The wind was light but the fresh air, scented lightly with mixtures of clover and honeysuckle, lifted her spirits.

"When's the last time you rode out here?" he asked.

She glanced at him. He looked so good in the saddle—always had. Trip was just the epitome of the perfect cowboy. His hat sat low over his brow, his back was straight, and he moved with the horse in a smooth, easy way. He fit out here in every way. Her heart longed for what could have been, for what she'd hoped could be at one time. She looked away and concentrated on what he'd said.

"It's been too long. I was here, you know, the month before Daddy died. I thank God every day that I came home that weekend. I'd needed to come for some time, but work was busy and, well, he and I had had a fight. I finally came home anyway and..." She paused, realizing she was rambling and hadn't answered his question. "I didn't take time to ride that weekend. And since I've been home, well, you know I've been busy going over the books and trying to get a hold on the business. The few times I've ridden in the round pen are all I've taken time for."

She shot him an embarrassed glance, and he nodded. She felt so guilty for having not come home.

"You said you didn't want to talk about the horse theft, but do you want to talk about anything else? Like why you were mad at your dad? None of my business, I know, but I'm here if you need a sounding board. I seem to remember we used to do that pretty well for each other."

Her heart cinched tight, and she swallowed hard as her throat suddenly ached with the want to talk like old times. She rested her wrist on the saddle horn, and held the reins lightly with her fingers and tried to relax, letting the feel of the horse's walk ease through her. She was so wound up she struggled to let go.

"I struggle…" she admitted at last. "Struggle with the fact that I wasn't here. And that he died thinking I was never coming home to live on the ranch he'd built for me."

At her revelation, Trip pulled his horse to a halt, and she did the same.

"Never? You don't plan to make Calhoun Ranch

your home—*ever*? I don't get that."

She looked down, the struggle real inside her. "I'm not sure anymore. I'm dealing with a lot right now."

And she was. Part of that involved Trip. But she couldn't tell him that.

CHAPTER FIVE

Trip had noticed she hadn't been around but once between the time he'd started working and Ray had died. His own father had told him that Ray and Lori had had an argument, but that Ray had been very close-mouthed about it and it had hit him hard. By the time Trip had agreed to work for Ray, the rancher had seemed set on his plan of action where Trip was concerned. Trip hadn't realized Ray was actually setting him up to run the ranch because he knew Lori was never going to take control.

The idea was hard-hitting and wrong. He stared at

her. "I don't get this. You always wanted to run this ranch. You and your dad talked about it for as long as I can remember. What happened?" Maybe he shouldn't ask but he couldn't help it.

"Things…change. Daddy said he wanted me to stretch my wings and try new things. He said it would be good for me and so I went. But then he decided he wanted me to come back home. But I had commitments. And I enjoyed working with the marketing firm and I wasn't ready. He took that as I was never coming home and he put pressure on me. I rebelled." She shifted in the saddle; it creaked with the movement. "I'm very much like him, you know. Stubborn and hardheaded as they come, and independent. And so he pushed my buttons, and I buried my feet in the dirt and took a stance like a stubborn horse determined not to budge for the trainer. I was okay about coming home on my terms, but not to be ruled and led by Daddy. I loved him so much, but I got scared that he wanted to control too much of my life. And so I stayed away."

He could understand her thinking. Ray was strong-willed, but she was right—so was she. It would be hard for them not to clash eventually. But— "I'm actually shocked you planned to stay away even if you and your dad fought. I never thought you would do anything but come back to the ranch. I mean, your dad told me you planned to stay at your job in marketing a little longer, but I didn't think…" He paused. "I don't think he believed you wouldn't be back."

She blinked hard, tears glistening in her eyes before she dashed them away with her fingertips. "It's been five months and I seem to always be close to tears these days. I know that's what he thought." Her voice cracked. "And then he hired you and demanded that I come home that weekend. Thankfully I did, and he explained what he was doing, but I had no idea a month later he'd be gone."

She urged her horse to start moving again and Trip did too. They were approaching the gate, and he moved ahead of her to lean down and opened it from the saddle. They rode through and he held back and then closed it. He took his time hoping to give her a moment to collect her emotions. She was a strong, independent woman; she was just vulnerable right now. But she would pull through.

He was troubled by what he'd heard.

He loped to catch up to her and his heart cinched when she glanced over her shoulder at him as he approached. Then she nudged her horse into a trot and then took off at a gallop.

Trip laughed and took off after her. She needed this. There was freedom galloping across an open pasture, especially when you were feeling hemmed in or down—and Lori had to be feeling both.

Bluebonnets were blooming as they raced over a hill of them and down the slope toward a gurgling creek that wove through the ranch. In their early years, they raced this path many times. Lori and her horse always jumped the creek to the other side. He wondered whether she'd do it now. He wondered how long it had been since she'd let herself run truly free like this.

He watched as she made her approach and knew the mare she was riding could make it. When she leaned low and didn't slow, he knew she was going for it. She rode the horse as effortlessly as she'd always ridden and easily jumped the water. When her horse landed, Lori stayed in the saddle perfectly and guided her horse back to face him. She was smiling brilliantly and nearly knocked him out of his saddle—she was so beautiful and looked happy. He urged his gelding forward and took the leap too, felt the power of the horse as it sprang forward and sailed easily to the other side. Laughing, he pulled up and his horse pranced a bit as it settled down.

"You couldn't resist." He smiled.

Her eyes flashed with happiness. "I know, I couldn't. It just felt good."

They dismounted and allowed their horses to get a drink from the clear creek. It was an old routine they'd done so many times growing up together when things had been good between them. He let go of the reins, knowing Jep and Bell weren't going anywhere.

The mesquite trees and the oaks were thick farther down the creek, but here the land was clear and perfect for enjoying a picnic or fishing. Or, as they'd done many times, wading in the shallow water.

"Are you going to pull off your boots and roll up your pants for a wade in the creek?" he asked.

She placed her hands on her hips and thought about it. "No, not today, I don't think. But maybe another day."

He moved to stand beside her and they watched the horses enjoy the water.

"So, there will be another time? Are you planning to stay?"

"We used to love coming here," she said, her voice smiling.

"Yes, we did." He didn't tell her that there wasn't a time that he rode by this spot and didn't think of her.

She smiled. "I remember when I was about eleven, you fell in."

"I was twelve, and you pushed me in." He scowled and then laughed.

"Oh, is that what happened," she teased. "I don't seem to recall it that same way."

He grunted. "Recall it however you want, but you pushed me that day." He laughed, knowing full well that she knew exactly what happened that day.

"If you say so. But I'll never admit that."

"I know."

"But you got me back," she accused. "I came in to help you up and you pulled me in with you."

He grinned, remembering. "You jumped up faster than a jackrabbit running from a rattlesnake. You were drenched and laughing..." *And beautiful.* His heart swelled because that had been the first time he'd noticed his friend as more. That had been the beginning for him, for the adolescent longing for more and too scared to let her know it. "I've missed you, Lori," he said, unable to stop the admission.

She inhaled slowly. "I've missed you too. We were a good pair back then."

"I think your dad knew we'd be a good pair again."

She looked at him then, and something sparked in her eyes. Something that sent his pulse careening. As quick as the heated gaze met his, she extinguished the flame and hid it behind blank eyes.

"Why did you pull away from me your senior year? You just closed me out. And then you left."

And there it was. The question that hung between them that she'd never asked…that he'd tried to avoid.

"You were the boss's daughter. I was the manager's son. And—" He halted, uncertain whether this was the right move to make but certain it was time to be open with her. "As kids that was fine, but then we weren't kids anymore."

She startled him when she stepped toward him, her expression confused. "I was always your friend, no matter what. I made a mistake letting you know I cared for you that night. If I'd have known my admission was going to drive you away, I wouldn't have said anything. I never dreamed you would turn away from me."

"I'm sorry, Lori."

Her eyes filled with pain. "You walked away and found new friends and left me hanging. And then you left for college and barely acknowledged me before you left."

"We don't need to open this up." He had wanted so many times to let his guard down with her, to step back across the line he'd drawn in the dirt between them after his dad had told him that his manager's job could be in jeopardy if Trip got romantically involved with Lori. Going away to school had been the right excuse.

"No, I think now is a good time to open it up." She lifted her chin stubbornly. "I'm about done, I think, with unanswered questions. I cared for you and you shunned me. It hurt and I think I deserve to know."

It took everything he had in him not to reach for her. She was only a step away from him and the fierce hurt mingled with fire and accusation pushed him to his limits. "I never meant to hurt you. I did what I had to do."

"Too bad—you did hurt me. I cared for you," she gritted out.

"I cared for you too. Lori, you were the boss's daughter. I had nothing to offer you."

She recoiled as if he'd slapped her. His heart thundered. "You had everything to offer me."

"What? I owned nothing; you owned a ranch. I was the ranch hand. Do you know what people would have said if I'd dared to be more than your friend?

They'd have said I was trying to move up in the world by using you."

Her jaw locked in place and her eyes glittered. "So you walked away and closed me out so people wouldn't talk? People are always going to talk and I couldn't care less."

"But I couldn't let them talk like that. I couldn't be that guy. And then there was the fact that my dad was afraid if I let my feelings be known and we broke up, his job could be on the line."

She laughed. "Daddy wouldn't have done that. And neither would I."

"It wouldn't have worked."

"Funny, I never took you for a coward."

He sucked in a sharp breath. "I'm not a coward. I did what I had to do."

"Oh really? You just assumed if we, you and I, explored the feelings we had for each other outside of being friends, that we wouldn't make it? And that I would think less of you because my daddy had a ranch?"

"A ranch that was going to be yours."

She glared at him. "In my heart of hearts, I knew that was why you pulled away from me." She swung around and strode to her horse. In one swift movement, she swept up the reins, grabbed the saddle horn and stepped into the stirrup, and then settled into the saddle.

"This ranch turned into a deficit to me after you left. It cost me you and now it's cost me my dad." She tore her eyes off him and glared at the surrounding beauty. A frown hardened her face. "It's too much."

He watched as she rode her horse through the stream and up the shallow bank, and then sent the horse into a gallop back toward home.

Trip didn't move. Couldn't move. He just watched her ride away.

Was he a coward?

Had he taken everyone's reactions for granted because his dad had?

And what was holding him back now?

CHAPTER SIX

Anger drove Lori to ride straight home and not look back. She didn't care whether Trip followed or not. She'd pushed the anger at him down deep; she had to or it would have driven her crazy. She hadn't even acknowledged until that moment that she'd resented the ranch. Oh, she'd felt it after Trip had pulled away, because she'd known that had to be part of it. She had ears and she'd heard other boys tease him, that he should grow up and marry her because she and the ranch were a package deal. But he'd just been her friend and had told them to lay off.

But in the end, the digs had hit their target.

And she could try to deny it all she wanted, but she and the ranch *were* a package deal. And the ranch was worth a lot…enough to run a man like Trip off.

She handed her horse over to one of the ranch hands as soon as she got back to the stable, then headed to the house. She did not want to talk to Trip any more today.

The office phone was ringing as she entered, jolting her from her thoughts. Glad for the distraction, she grabbed the phone from its dock and answered it immediately.

"Lori, this is Madge Clark, the secretary at the Oklahoma Buckout Rodeo. I need to have a word with you."

Dread filled her. "Sure, what can I do for you?" She'd been waiting for this call.

The Buckout had specifically booked her top five horses. And they were missing. She'd wondered how long she'd have before they'd hear the news and call. Obviously word was out.

Madge didn't waste time. "As you know, our

event is with the top-ranked saddle broncs. And, well, we've heard Cimarron Trouble and your other top four horses are missing. Have you got any news on them?"

"None so far. We've got the Knight Agency looking into it, as well as the Texas and Southwestern Cattle Raisers Association because we've also had some cattle stolen."

"Good. If anyone can locate them, the TSCRA or the Knight Agency can. Do you have any leads? We hate this for you. But as much as I hate it, if your top five can't show up then we have to bring in the next in rank to fill in."

Lori rubbed her temple, feeling a headache coming on. Her entire body tensed. "In all honesty, Madge, we have no leads at this point. We don't even have a motive other than what they're worth. But they're branded and it will sure be hard for them to be sold. So it's going to be hard for someone to get by with this as far as I can see."

"I think so too. But if they aren't found, then I'll have to let Stan Kramer's stock fill the slots since they rank above your other horses. That's how we do this event."

Lori's heart sank. This was what she'd feared. To make it to the finals, her horses needed this rodeo. "Can you give me at least until after Fort Worth before you cancel?"

"We can do that. And I wish you the best of luck. I'll contact you soon after Fort Worth."

Lori leaned her head back against her dad's chair and closed her eyes. "Okay, fair enough." They ended the call and Lori pushed out of the chair and paced the office.

She stopped to stare out the window and saw Trip heading to his truck. She needed to tell him the news, but not right now. She just couldn't handle facing him again today. Not after having lost it out there like she'd done.

No matter what was between them, they were going to have to run the ranch together or she was going to need to go back to Houston. And frankly, she no longer knew what it was she wanted to do.

But for tonight, she was going to relax in a warm bath, listen to a book on tape, and try really hard to escape everything around her for a few hours. And if she was lucky, she'd sleep and wake up ready to face another day.

The morning after their fight, Trip, tired and in a less than happy mood from lack of sleep and concern over the way things were going, headed to see Lori. His men had quickly gotten out of his way and headed off to their various jobs for the day, including Harvey. The man was irritating and obviously looking for ways to lose his job. Trip hadn't figured out why the man was still here but he was watching him. And he wasn't firing him—not yet, anyway.

Mike, on the other hand, continued to apologize for leaving the trailer, and the kid worked harder than everyone else, trying to keep his job. Trip figured he'd just done what he was told to do the night the trailer load of horses was stolen.

Trip's friend, Vance Presley, had called this morning and said they'd had rustlers on their pastures that bordered Lori's ranch. Trip had made a decision as he'd hung the phone up and headed to find Lori. They might have their problems, but he was still her foreman and needed to do his job. He was walking out of the stables when he saw Lori come out of the house. His gut clenched as she came his way.

Yesterday, he'd hurt for her and he hurt for the pain he'd put her through. But he didn't, in all good conscience, believe now was the time to place any other kind of pressure on her by hashing out their past and their future. Any hope of getting past the resentment she felt about everything had been hit hard yesterday. He'd left her alone after their ride, deciding they both needed time to pull back, despite every fiber of his being wanting to go after her.

"I have news." She halted at the tailgate of his truck, keeping distance between them. She looked weary, as if she hadn't slept either.

"What's happened?"

"I got a call about the Buckout. If we can't recover our horses within a few days after Fort Worth is over, they're going to give the contract to Stan Kramer."

He grimaced. "I was afraid of this. If Kramer wasn't such a jerk I wouldn't mind it so much. But the guy is a jerk. A big one."

"How do you mean? I don't know him. He must have come on the scene while I was away."

"Let's just say he's not my favorite person. We're going to find your horses," he said, more determined than ever to get them back.

"Our horses. You are just as much an owner as I am."

He nodded, seeing the impersonal glint in her eyes and not liking it at all. He wanted to see that spark of connection that was usually there, despite her fight not to let it show. This morning the light was out, and it disturbed him more than anything. But clearly she was trying, like he was, to get back to the impersonal footing they'd been teetering on before the ride yesterday.

"Yeah, I know. We're going to find them. I wanted to run an idea by you. I'm not willing to trust anyone who works here at the moment, and decided to let the Presleys in on what's going on. I think we need some extra ears at Fort Worth. And, frankly, around here too. Your dad hired me to look out for your interests and that's what I plan to do. That being said, I want to bring Vance and his family into the fold on this. If you agree."

If there was anyone he knew he could trust, it was Vance and his dad and four brothers. Marcus, the father, had been Ray Calhoun's best friend. He would have trusted them too.

"Sure, I trust them completely. I'm actually startled Marcus hasn't called to check on me, but I think they were in Florida last week for Lana's wedding, so they've been busy."

"Yes, that's where they were but they're home. And Vance called and said they had cattle stolen out of the pastures sharing a fence with you. I thought I'd ride over there and talk to them about it. About all of it."

"Rustlers—I'm sick of them," she snapped. Her pretty face twisted with disgust. "What do you have in mind? I'm all in and going over there with you."

Trip hated this. For a moment yesterday, they'd almost turned back time to the way they'd once been. He wanted that back...

He just wasn't sure there was any way to ever get back there again.

For now, he had a job to do.

CHAPTER SEVEN

Lori struggled to remain unaffected by Trip. But she was. She should have been over this years ago, but she'd held it in for so long that, despite everything, he had an effect on her.

"Vance is riding in the saddle bronc competition and I want to see if he'll be on the lookout and listen for anything that seems suspicious. And all of them would do anything to help you."

It was true. The Presleys had always been her neighbors. Five boys and one girl. Lana had been one of her friends growing up and had just married. The guys, as far as she knew, were all still single and running the ranch.

"So you want to head over there now and see who is around?"

"Sure." They climbed into the truck. She could feel Trip slide a glance her way several times as he drove. He was not going to bring up their fight from the day before. She wasn't either. She was going to let it ride and sink back into the dark.

Vance and Drake were the first Presleys they saw as they drove up to the arenas. They were looking over a group of horses in the round pen. She saw Brice and Shane riding across the pasture some distance out.

"Hey, little girl," Drake said, grinning with that slightly crooked smile and twinkling eyes.

She laughed as he gave her a big hug. They'd seen each other several times since she'd been home, always offering her any help she needed. Drake was the oldest of the kids and had always liked to tease her and Lana. Who was she kidding? They all teased her and Lana.

"You look tired." Vance studied her as he gave her

a quick hug.

"I'm fine." She glanced at Trip. "How was Lana's wedding?"

Drake looked pleased. "It was great. Lana will be moving back to Texas after the honeymoon so we're very happy about that."

"Cam's got a ranch over toward Henderson," Vance added. "And he's a good guy. His family owns the resort on Windswept Bay. It was nice. Not that I'm into the beach myself, but Lana liked it."

Cooper overheard the conversation and strode up. "But we're glad she met a cowboy who is bringing her back to Texas. That place is beautiful but Lana belongs in Texas." He grinned and then also gave Lori a quick hug. "Good to see you, stranger."

"Stranger? I saw you last week at the diner having dinner with a pretty blonde."

He grinned. "Well, you won't marry me so I have to keep looking."

She laughed. "Right."

Cooper was a flirt. He shot Trip a look. "You need to take Lori to that new place in town. It's nice, and the

73

food is great."

Trip met her gaze and her insides warmed. "Maybe I'll do that," he said, startling her. "But first, we came to ask for your help. Did you hear Lori had her top-ranked horses taken from the Mesquite rodeo? I figure the news is just starting to get out but y'all were busy with the wedding and all."

"Do what?" Vance growled.

"Who?" Cooper snapped. "This rustling is out of hand,"

Brice and Shane rode up on their horses just in time to hear what was said.

"No kidding," Brice said, his serious gaze blazing.

"I'm sick of it," Shane said, shaking his head, a look of disgust on his handsome face.

They dismounted and both gave her a hug.

"Now what's going on?" Shane asked.

Trip repeated what had happened.

Drake spoke first. "We had a load go missing while we were gone. We were just about to address the problem. You had a load go missing last week, right? And now these horses. I've called TSCRA and alerted them."

"We've done it too. And the Knight Agency is looking into the horses since it happened at a WRC-sanctioned rodeo."

"Do you think they're related incidents?" Vance asked.

Trip shrugged. "We're waiting on an update from them today. But I'm not sure if the two are related or not. The deal is we don't know who to trust. It could be an inside job from someone on the ranch, as it often is. Or your ranch. And then the rodeo—who knows? We don't want to accuse the two men who were responsible for the trailer of horses, but Sean Knight is suspicious. He's the brother who came out the day after it happened and looked around and asked questions. It could also be personal. We let some men go when Lori took over the ranch."

Drake stared hard from one to the other. "So what do you plan to do? And what do we need to do?"

"Right," Coop said. "Whatever you need, we're here to help."

Five tough cowboys stepped forward to flank Trip

and six pairs of eyes focused on Lori. Her knees went weak at the powerful show of support.

"There you go," Trip said. "Your own posse."

Marcus Presley's black Dodge truck drove up the lane and crossed the gravel yard to come to a halt in front of them. Marcus climbed out and strode toward them, clearly concerned as he looked at the group. "What's up? Lori, I just got a call from a friend who told me you had horses stolen in Mesquite?"

"And leave it to Dad to be the one who hears the news." Drake gave a dry laugh.

Marcus hugged her and looked down at her before he let her go. "Have you come to let us in on this, darlin'?" he asked. "Because you know we're not going to stand for this."

"Thanks, Marcus. Yes, we've been telling the guys about it. And we're about to try to get together a plan of action."

He let her go. "Good. Glad I got here when I did."

Trip filled Marcus in and then looked at Vance. "You'll be in Fort Worth riding in the saddle broncs and I was hoping that you could keep your ears open for anyone saying anything that might seem suspicious."

Vance gave a curt nod of his Stetson. "I will be glad too."

"Great. If you notice anybody who you think shouldn't be there slipping around behind the scenes or around the trailers, let us know. Someone may be planning to steal someone else's stock. Lori might not be the only target."

"True," Drake agreed.

"If I think anything is off, I'll say so," Vance said quickly. "I'm all in."

His brothers echoed his sentiment.

"Carson would be here to back you up too," Cooper added, looking at Lori. "But his ex is giving him fits and he's dealing with that. But he sent his good wishes."

"Tell him thanks," Lori added. "Y'all are the best friends a girl could have."

"You're pretty special to us, Lori. I believe the rest of us can make the rodeo under the guise of watching Vance compete," Marcus said. "But the reality is we'll be mingling and asking questions."

"Let's do it," Cooper said, and all his brothers agreed.

Lori was overwhelmed again by their support. "You guys are going to make me cry. I mean, this is just too much to ask."

Trip put his arm around her and pulled her into his side, giving her a gentle hug. His action touched her deeply and made their fight the day before seem small.

Drake smiled. "It's what friends are for, you know?"

"Yes, and I'm so blessed to have all of you. Daddy is smiling right now, I'm sure."

Marcus grinned. "He'd be haunting us if we weren't helping you."

"You're probably right." She laughed, as did everyone, because her dad had been so strong-willed and it fit his personality. She missed him so much but felt him there with her, surrounded by this wonderful support network of friends.

With a plan in place, she and Trip headed home.

"You're not alone," Trip said quietly as they

started driving.

"I know." She had good neighbors and friends, and it helped to know that she had all those strong, great cowboys with her. "Thank you, Trip. We have some past that we need to let go of, I agree. But Daddy knew what he was doing when he worked so hard to hire you back on as manager. I'm sorry I was so mad yesterday."

He took his right hand off the steering wheel and took her hand, but kept his eyes straight ahead as he drove.

"The reality is you had a right to be." He slowed the truck on the quiet country road and turned to face her. "Lori, I'm sorry. We're...complicated, I'll admit that. But you need to know that I'm here for you, just like the Presleys are. I can't guarantee you'll get your horses back before Oklahoma, but if they're still alive and breathing out there, we will find them. I promise."

She believed him. His words meant a lot. "I think so too. Thank you." His hand on hers felt so good. Since her dad died, she'd felt alone and distant, but right then she didn't.

She turned her hand over so that their palms touched. She wrapped her fingers around his and squeezed tightly; he squeezed back. Butterflies lifted and fluttered through her chest, taking light to all the dark corners of her heart.

And that scared her to death because now her heart was opened up to being broken once again.

Trip's heart raced all the way to the ranch, and it was all he could do not to pull Lori into his arms and kiss her like he'd always dreamed of doing. But he didn't need to do that right now. She just needed him to do his job and be there for her for now. She was still adjusting to losing her dad. And then losing the horses on top of that. She'd had too many things to deal with right now. But that didn't make it any easier on him.

As he stopped in front of the ranch house, his phone rang. "It's Jesse Knight. He's the last one of the brothers I talked to. I'll come into the house with you so we can take this together."

She nodded and got out. He answered the call as

he followed her up the walk and into the house. "Hey, Jesse. Good to hear from you." He followed Lori into the office.

"I have some news."

"Great. Lori's here with me in her office. I'll put you on speakerphone."

"That's good," Jesse said. "Hi, Lori. I think you both might be interested in something we've dug up. Your man, Harvey, once worked for Kramer Stock. Did you know that? I figure since Lori just got involved with the ranch workings again that she wouldn't know, but maybe you knew, Trip?"

Trip frowned. "No, I didn't know. He was here during my dad's time as manager but I think Ray hired him. He's been less than cooperative since the horses were stolen." Trip didn't like it. "Though we've taken precautions on the hunch that it could be an inside job, I've been holding out hope that it wouldn't be."

"Me too." Lori looked pained by the news.

"I get that," Jesse agreed. "But this doesn't look good. Stan Kramer doesn't have the best reputation out there among other rodeo stock contractors, but it's undeniable that he does have some bucking stock moving up the ranks."

"Tell me about it," Trip grunted. He'd had his run-ins with Kramer. "His horses might buck good, but I question his treatment of them. And we had a horse colic the month after I took this job. I couldn't pin it on Kramer but we had suspicions about them tampering with our feed. And it just happened that his horse got to fill the spot on the ticket when we had to pull out."

Lori's eyes widened. "Did Dad suspect him of tampering with the horse feed?"

"He did. But to steal a trailer full of horses would be bold of him. Since his five automatically would fill the ticket, it seems a little bold."

"Yes," Jesse agreed. "But if he was desperate, he might do it."

Trip's adrenaline spiked. "And is he?"

"Sean, Michael, and I believe he could be. We've got a source that says the bank is on his heels hard. And my wife, Carly, also has had her own run-in with the man with her stock contracting company. She's not surprised by any of this either. We've quietly opened an investigation into Kramer's dealings and wanted to let you know."

"So what should we do about Harvey?" Trip asked. But his gut told him the man was too sensitive about being questioned.

"Don't do anything for now. Let us dig deeper. But it goes without saying that you need to keep your eyes open. And we will all be in Fort Worth if possible. We've got several investigations going right now but we're zeroed in on this."

"Okay, thanks. We'll see you there," Trip said.

"Thanks, Jesse. I'm grateful for your help. See you in Fort Worth." She was frowning as he ended the call. "I hate this. I know Harvey has been defensive this whole time but I still don't want to believe it. He's been here for several years."

"Yeah, I hate it too. But my gut is telling me it isn't a coincidence. He's been testy ever since I signed on. Look, everyone is working cattle in the north section today and I need to go check on things. But then I'm going to check on the cattle in the south pastures near where the Presleys' cattle went missing. We may have been hit too and not know it yet."

"I'll come too. I'm sick of this, Trip. And I'm

done feeling lost in all of this. This is my ranch and someone has a reckoning coming if they think I'm an easy mark."

Trip couldn't help smiling. He saw the spark of fire in her eyes. "I like that fire in your eyes, Lori Calhoun."

She laughed despite everything. "Thanks, if they want a fight, then I'm ready. This has been one evolution of a day for me. Now let's go check on the cattle. And then we'll come back and take a look at the books on our rough stock. I want to see the records on that sick horse you told Jesse about earlier. The one that got replaced by Kramer's horse. I know you and Daddy had plans to make our rough stock into the best program around and I want that too, Trip. Especially now."

"Especially now?" he questioned.

Her eyes twinkled. "Now that I've decided I'm not leaving. I'm making my stake here, Trip. Can you handle that?"

His heart slammed against his ribs. "I can handle it."

CHAPTER EIGHT

Later, they drove up to where the men were branding and vaccinating the herd of cattle. Before they had a chance to get out of the truck, Harvey galloped over on his horse to Trip's side of the truck and glared down at him.

"Do you not think I can handle working the cattle now?"

Lori's temper shot to the sun. "What did he say?" she hissed, not believing her ears. Trip reached out and put a hand on her arm. She kept silent.

"Harvey." Trip's hand gently squeezed her arm. "I have no doubt you can handle this, but our *boss* wanted to look at her cattle," Trip said with a calm voice edged in steel. "It has nothing to do with you. We're just here to watch for a minute. Then we're moving on."

"Right. Like I'll believe that." He whirled his horse around and galloped back to the cattle.

Trip got out of the truck and she did the same. She was fuming. "Who does he think he is?" she snapped.

"Hang on, boss." Trip chuckled. "I'm not sure what he thinks he's accomplishing but let it slide for now. I'm actually here to push his buttons. We want him to mess up. So I'm not going to take his bait. I'll have my moment."

"Fine. For now. But he's not making it easy."

He winked at her. "Patience. For a few minutes. Then we'll head out to the other pastures to check on the other herd."

"Okay, go for it. But I'm not feeling particularly forgiving at the moment, so he better not cross me."

He chuckled. "Feisty. I like it."

Lori was hotter than she could remember ever being when they got back in the truck and headed across the pastures to the far side of the ranch. The fact that

Harvey could be so belligerent and probably responsible for taking or helping steal her horses got under her skin like a hot poker. She hadn't been this angry since the year Trip pulled away from her and went another direction from their friendship and the future she'd hoped to have with him.

But she was moving on from that and pushed that aside. She could not keep going back to the past. She had to let it go and focus on the here and now. On the ranch. Harvey might very well be messing with the legacy her father built for her and also with the business that she and Trip shared. And if he wasn't the culprit, then he was not doing himself any favors with his behavior.

"You doing okay over there?" Trip asked finally. "You cooling off any? I could tell you were about to blow a gasket back there."

"Harvey has a chip on his shoulder. And it's not just about the horse trailer stock gone missing. His behavior is bizarre and I just can't take it."

Trip shot her a narrowed glance. "But you did good. We didn't need to make him think we have any suspicions. Let him be that way. I'm going to nail him if he stole those horses."

"I'm with you—just furious at the moment. I have a hunch that he thought the manager's position was his. I think he has a grudge against my dad, which would mean the ranch and me and you also because you got the job he thought my dad was going to give to him."

"I think you might be right but we will see. Soon."

"I hope so. Maybe they'll slip up and the Knights will dig up something more on them too. Or who knows, maybe we'll catch them. I'm looking forward to catching them. Honestly, I'm angrier about this than I've been in a very long time. I'm as mad as I was when you put distance between us and found new friends, then left for college—" The words just flowed before she had time to stop them.

Trip went still. His hands tightened on the steering wheel and his jaw muscle flexed with tension, but he didn't look at her. Didn't say anything.

Maybe getting how angry she'd been out in the open was a good thing. Trip had had his reasons for doing what he did, which she didn't completely understand, but that didn't diminish how hurt she'd been. Wounded.

Still, the little voice of reason in her head reminded her that while he'd been her friend, he'd never said he loved her. He had no obligation to her back then or now. And she needed to come to grips with that fact.

It didn't matter whether she'd loved him because that fact didn't mean he had any obligation to her whatsoever.

She bit her lip as the war in her head and heart waged on. She glanced at him but he stared straight ahead, as tense as she'd ever seen him.

They'd reached the ranch boundary fence and she saw the cattle at the bottom of the hill. Trip stopped the truck and rammed the gear into park. Tension filled the cab like a thick fog. He pushed open his door and got out, slamming it behind him.

It hit her then exactly how upset he was. Maybe she'd gone too far. Heart thundering, she went after him.

CHAPTER NINE

Trip could barely think straight. He told himself to calm down but clearly Lori didn't get what he had gone through when he'd pulled away from her. He couldn't take it anymore. He strode around the front of the truck and she met him. Pain was in her eyes.

"Trip, I didn't mean to bring that up agai—"

"Lori, I had nothing to offer you. It didn't mean I didn't want you..." He pulled her into his arms and saw her eyes flare wide just before he covered her mouth with his.

He heard her small gasp and then she melted into

him. Her arms went around him and she responded to his kiss. He loved her with a depth she had no idea about, but it was true.

He felt her heart pounding against his own, felt the curve of her body against him and the softness of her lips moving beneath his. He broke the kiss, needing to pull back. "Lori, I'm warning you, when we find our horses, I plan to move forward, not backward. I love you, always have."

Tears filled her eyes.

"Don't cry. I don't ever want to hurt you again. I only want to make you smile."

She smiled gently. "I may never stop smiling now."

"And then I'll be a happy man." He smiled.

She kissed his lips gently. "I love you and thank you for opening up to me."

"I couldn't stand to see you hurting because of something I did. I just thought I needed to give you time to heal from your grief, and then the horses got stolen and I didn't want to add any more stress to you. But by holding back, I realized I was adding to your stress."

She laid her head against his chest. "Daddy isn't coming back. And I'm coming to terms with that and I'll always miss him. But feeling so alone was the hardest thing. And then, after having adjusted somewhat over time to losing you, I had to come back here, feeling alone, and try to work with you every day and not be affected...it only intensified everything."

His arms tightened around her. "You're not alone, darlin'. I'm here for you. And it feels so good to have you in my arms." He rested his head against hers and they held each other.

She sighed and opened her eyes, looking across the land they'd roamed together as kids. "I have so many memories of us, running wild all over this ranch together. It feels so right to have you here with me."

"I'm thrilled to be here with you."

Her gaze rested on the knee-tall grass. "Are those tracks?" She lifted her head from his chest.

"Where?"

She pointed a few feet away.

Trip released her and moved to where the grass

was bent down. "Yes, it is. And I haven't had men over here for a couple of days. I think we've had unwanted visitors."

Trip's mind whirled. "I have a suspicion that someone was scouting your herd. Rustlers took cattle from the Presleys next door and checked yours out the same night. From what Vance said, they took a trailer load so they probably plan to come back for these. Soon."

"We need to do a stakeout," Lori snapped, anger on her pretty face. "I'm so done with this."

He smiled, despite everything. "Me too. I'm going to spend the next few nights on stakeout, watching and waiting." He strode farther down the hill, following the tracks through the tall weeds.

Lori trudged beside him. "Me too."

"No, you will—"

"Be right here beside you. No way am I letting you do this alone."

"I'll get one of the Presleys to join me."

"I'm doing this," she said, stubborn as ever.

"Fine. But you'll stay out of the way. I'm not letting you get hurt."

She crossed her arms. "I'm capable of taking care of myself. I'll bring my rifle."

Stubborn woman. "I'm going to call Jesse back and let him know what's going on. Let's go if we're going to get ready and be back here before it's too late."

Now, if he could just keep her safe, everything would be fine.

CHAPTER TEN

It was a cloudy night as Trip parked the truck in a stand of mesquite trees along the creek. He cut the lights and he and Lori settled in to wait.

Ever since Trip had opened up to her that afternoon and kissed her, Lori had been floating on a cloud.

Now, sitting in the truck with him, she could hardly believe it. *He'd told her he loved her.* She was finding it hard to concentrate on anything other than that fact.

She waited all these years—it seemed as if she had

been waiting all of her life to hear Trip tell her that he loved her. And now he had.

Now they needed to get through all of this junk with the ranch, get past this rustling and find their horses and put an end to all this nonsense so that the stock company could be a success. She understood that he needed that. Trip was the kind of man who had to bring something to the table.

But she'd needed something too, needed him to open up to her like he'd done today. There was an ache inside her that his words had soothed, had vanquished. The ache was gone because he *loved* her and that was the most valuable thing in the world to her. Now that she had that, she didn't care whether someone came and stole every cow or horse she owned. She had everything she needed with Trip's love.

But understanding what he needed drove the fire inside her to stay out here and wait and watch, and try to catch whoever was doing this. They needed to see whether the rustlers stealing the cattle were the same ones who'd taken her horses. For the sake of the ranch, the stock company, and Trip.

In the darkness, he reached out and took her hand. The thrill went through her as his warm, callused hand wrapped around hers. He interlaced his fingers with hers and there they sat.

It was midnight. They had a busy day tomorrow, as the horses would be loaded in the morning and taken the three-hour drive to Fort Worth. The rodeo would start in the evening. They were both going to be worn out.

She yawned. "If they're coming, I wish they would come now so we can find out who they are and catch them, and then we can go and sleep a little. We are going to be so tired tomorrow night at the rodeo."

He chuckled. "You're right about that. I don't think either of us slept last night. You can lie down and rest your head on my thigh and sleep. I'll let you know if they show up."

She squeezed his hand. "I'm not doing that. You'd probably sneak out and leave me snoring. Besides, I'm not abandoning you here in the truck while you have to stay awake and watch."

She felt his grin in the darkness. She could barely

see him because he'd cut all the dash lights off inside the truck.

"I'll be fine. You really should rest."

"And you really should remember that I'm not going to do that." As she was saying the words, she saw a light bob in the distance. "Do you see that?" she whispered, as if whoever was in the other truck could hear her talking.

"I see it. We have company."

"How many do you think it is?" She was still talking in a hushed voice.

"I don't know. We'll know soon enough. Whatever happens, stay behind me. I'd rather you stay in the truck, but I know that's not gonna happen."

"You *do* know me."

He gave a dry laugh. "I know you."

Before she realized what he was doing, he pulled her into his arms, cupped her face in the darkness and kissed her again. Butterflies, fireflies, and moths with fire-laced wings exploded through her chest. This kiss was different than that afternoon. It was hard and fast and almost desperate. It left her breathless when he pulled away. And wanting more.

"Lori." His voice was raspy. "I can't have anything happen to you. Do you understand that?"

"Yes. But I don't want anything happening to you."

"It won't. But you have to stay here. I'm going down there. You have to do as I ask. I mean it."

Her mouth went dry and her heart raced. "But this is my fight too."

"I understand that," he gritted in frustration. "Lori, I can handle this."

Indecision rolled in a long wave through her. "I'll go with you but stay back. You can't ask me to do less than that. "

"Fine. Have it your way." He kissed her quickly again and then let her go.

Tension radiated between them, different from what it was before, but it was there. She knew he wanted to keep her safe; however, there was no way she wasn't going down there. They rolled their windows down and they could hear the low whine of the truck as it came across the pastures. It topped the hill and they could make out the outline of a truck and trailer.

They had come after their cattle. There was no doubt about it. They had scouted it the other night and now they had come back to take what they wanted. *Or try to*, Lori thought.

Trip got out of the truck. She slid over and followed him out the same door. He reached back inside and took his rifle from the gun rack on the back window. Lori wished she had brought hers—not that she'd ever used it for anything but target practice and shooting poisonous snakes. But she figured if she needed to protect herself or someone she loved, she'd be able to take care of business. But no, she'd let him talk her out of it. "I wish I had my gun."

"You're not going to need your gun. I have mine, but it's okay—you're going to stay back. Remember?"

"Right."

Frustrations of her own had her shifting from one boot to the other as they watched the trailer lights showing them exactly where the truck was going. They crept through the tall grass and she was thankful for her boots, as she didn't relish the idea of stepping on any creepy snakes tonight. She might scream and that wouldn't be good.

They were half a football field length away when Trip stopped moving unexpectedly and she slammed into the back of him.

"Umph," she grunted and then squeaked, "Sorry."

They waited, as they could make out two men unloading horses. Of course they'd brought horses. That was one thing about cattle rustling: rustlers had to know what they were doing when they stole cattle. They had to know how to cut what they wanted from the herd, and how to load them. It wasn't a skill set that everyone had. Which meant that a cattle rustler was normally a cowboy.

When the two mounted their horses and rode toward the herd, Trip leaned back and whispered, "Let's go."

He started across the pasture again, keeping low as they took a parallel path down the hill and advanced toward the truck. Her adrenaline was high as she followed Trip.

And prayed that nothing went wrong.

Trip knew Brice and Cooper were out there somewhere, on the lookout for rustlers on their property. And so were Shane and Drake. Vance had stayed home after much persuasion so he'd be fit to compete tomorrow night. He was in the running to make it to the finals again and he couldn't miss that opportunity.

There was a lot of ranch to watch over and he hoped they made it here before anything bad went down. He'd sent them a text but had no idea how far away they were.

Shane and Drake would stay home tomorrow night and keep watch on the ranch, looking for rustlers while everyone else tried to help at the rodeo.

They all understood that the rustlers had scouted the ranches and would be back quickly before the cattle were moved out of the pastures they'd been in when the rustlers had scoped them out.

Worry knotted in his gut for the stubborn,

beautiful woman following him like a shadow. *If he couldn't keep her safe...* Even the thought of it had his stomach churning. *He would keep her safe.*

He leaned close to Lori. "I'm going in," he whispered. "You have your phone if something goes wrong. I need you to stay here and make the call to 911 now that we know they're really intending to steal the cattle."

"Okay, but I'm not promising that I'll stay here after I make the call. You take care of yourself."

"You better stay. You promised. Now make the call." He forced himself not to be distracted and then he made his way toward the rustlers. He thought there were four rustlers. Two on horses and two working the trailer.

He hoped these were the same people who'd taken the horses. If so, then maybe they'd get some answers. It was more important now than ever since he'd spilled his guts to Lori. He needed the stock to make it to the finals and let everyone know that the stock company was going to make it without the larger-than-life presence of Ray.

He needed to stand on his own if he was going to ask Lori to marry him. And he was going to ask her because he couldn't stand being apart from her any longer.

"Can we hurry this up," one of the men growled. "I got a bad feeling about this."

Trip reached the truck and hurried down the side of it and between the tailgate and the cattle trailer. He peeked around the edge. This close, he could see the two men.

"I'm all for getting this over with. Tell Carter and Lomax to sort and load faster."

Carter and Lomax…two of the ranch hands he'd let go for making unsavory remarks about Lori when she took over for her dad. He'd fired them on the spot. And now the no-goods were stealing her cattle. Trip's blood boiled as he listened to them.

"Hurry up," the second rustler snapped. "You two act like you never sorted cattle before."

In answer, Carter and Lomax cut two heifers from the herd and made them charge the two cowboys working their mouths more than the gate to the trailer.

"Hey, watch out!" Simon growled. The third

man's distinctive voice finally registered as he remembered the cowboy's name. He didn't think he knew the fourth rustler. But he would.

Trip moved silently down the side of the trailer. The cattle they'd just run up into the trailer made enough noise to drown out any he happened to make. Trip crouched low and moved quickly toward the man holding the trailer gate. He didn't stop until the barrel of his rifle was in Simon's back.

"What?"

"Nice and easy," Trip said. "And I won't have to hurt you. Now step out there. You too," he said to the other rustler.

"What do you think you're doing?" Simon asked, his voice hard.

"Getting you ready to go to jail. Now move. And call your buddies."

Suddenly there was movement and the loud crack of a bullwhip sounded. Instantly, the cattle stampeded straight toward the trailer. The cowboys on horseback knew exactly what they were doing. Trip slammed tight against the side of the trailer while Simon was hit head-on by one cow. He stumbled and went down, and was trampled by the first cow.

Trip yelled, "Yah." He waved his arms in hopes the cattle would see him in the darkness. He reached down to grasp Simon by the arm and drug him up and out of the way of the rest of the herd. The man was groaning and could barely stand. When the cattle had run past, Trip looked around, and in the pale light, he saw Lomax on horseback. He had a struggling, mad-as-a-hornet Lori laid over his saddle horn.

"Put me down," Lori yelled. She couldn't believe she'd let the rustler see her. But she'd been unable to stand it, hiding in the weeds, and had crept closer. And Ted Lomax had spotted her as she'd raced to get out of the path of the stampeding cattle. He'd ridden forward and yanked her up and across his horse like a sack of potatoes before she'd had a chance to scream.

"Hold still and I won't have to shoot your boyfriend."

"No! You wouldn't dare," she gasped. "You, you should know that I called the police and a whole posse is on the way." She thought of Trip calling the Presleys her posse. She knew they'd be out there somewhere. *Come on, posse.*

"Put your rifle down, Trip," he demanded, as if she hadn't spoken at all.

She shot Trip a warning glare. "Don't you dare put your rifle down, Trip," she yelled. "Lomax, y'all are stealing cattle. That's not a hanging offense any longer! But killing us is—this is ridiculous. Take my stinkin' cattle. But don't do this."

"She's right," Trip warned. "Don't make this any worse than it is. You can take the cattle. And you can even keep the five horses if you took them."

"I don't want to kill anyone," a man grunted.

Lori held her head up from where she dangled over the front shoulder of the horse. Simon, one of the men Trip had fired with Lomax. She bet Carter was out here too. "Good for you," she yelled.

"I was just in this to get back at them for firing us," he continued. "I don't want any part of killin'."

"Me either," another man yelled.

Lori couldn't see him and didn't recognize him.

She knew there was another man on horseback out here. She'd seen him when Lomax had grabbed her.

Now she saw him approaching. But in the dark, she couldn't see his face with his hat pulled low. But she'd bet that was Carter.

"Carter, take the rifle from Trip."

Suddenly, she saw the rider level his shotgun, but instead of pointing it at Trip, he shoved it into the unsuspecting Lomax's ribs.

"No can do—"

Lori gasped. *Cooper Presley* sat in the saddle.

"What?" Lomax growled.

"No ifs, ands, or buts," Coop drawled. "I'm a crack shot and a hothead. And you happen to have one of my very favorite females in all the world dumped over your horse in a very uncomfortable position. So, I'd think long and hard about what this shotgun can do at close range. And I'd toss that pistol you're holding over there to the side."

She heard the sound of hooves, and out of the darkness five more horses and riders moved in and flanked Lomax. They all leveled a firearm at the man sharing a horse with her.

Lomax said something vulgar and then tossed the pistol to the ground.

Instantly, Trip came to her and helped her scramble off the saddle horn. He pulled her into his arms and held her. "Are you okay?"

"I'm better now," she managed, and wrapped her arms around his neck as he carried her away from Lomax and his horse.

Later, as the police got there and took the four rustlers away Lori looked around the group of cowboys. Trip had his arm around her shoulders, holding her close. "Thank you all for showing up," she said, her heart full of love and gratitude to these wonderful men.

"Yeah, thanks to all of you," Trip said, hugging her close.

She stared at Cooper. "Cooper, that was a pretty good trick you did on the horse. I was so glad to see you."

His brothers all chuckled. The tension was gone at last and they were all relaxing a bit.

"You should have seen him," Vance said. "We had just reached the area when the cattle stampeded and he jumped out of the truck and streaked across the pasture and grabbed that rider off his horse before he knew what hit him. I had followed him and he handed him off to me, then swung up into the saddle and rode the horse back toward y'all like he was one of them."

The night was lit up with truck lights and so Cooper's cocky grin was visible. "Hey, I figured it was our best shot of getting close."

"And you were right," Marcus said. "So, they said they didn't know anything about the stolen horses. And they took our cattle just to throw everyone off, hoping no one would suspect them."

"Yes, that's what they said," Trip said. "So as unbelievable as it is, we had cattle rustlers and horse thieves at the same time."

"That is beating the odds on bad luck." Drake shook his head. "Any more news from the Knights?"

"I'll call them in the morning and tell them what happened, and I'll see if there is any more news. They'll all be at the stockyards. Speaking of that, I guess we better all call it a night. Lori, let's get you home."

"Okay. I'm too wound up to sleep, but maybe I can. Thanks again, fellas. I'm a lucky woman to have all of you."

And she was. When they reached the ranch, Trip walked her to her door and held her. "I don't want to let you go," he said against her temple.

"I know. I love you. I was so scared when they were threatening to shoot you."

"And I was terrified when I saw they had you. I don't want to ever lose you, Lori."

"I love hearing you say that. You won't."

And she went to bed that night with that thought on her mind.

CHAPTER ELEVEN

As planned, they drove the horses to the Fort Worth Stockyards, checked them in, and then met with the Knights in the lobby of the historic Stockyard Hotel. Lori loved the old hotel; she'd spent many nights in this hotel when she and her dad came to the Stockyards. She loved the history of the place and the beautiful furnishings. She loved the way the old stairs creaked when she walked up them and she found the ancient, slow-moving elevator fascinating as a kid.

It was the perfect place to meet because her dad had loved it too. She sighed; it felt as if he was sitting beside her at the meeting.

Only two of the Knight brothers had come: Jesse, the ex-military policeman, and then Sean, the veterinarian who took care of the rodeo stock while at the events. After they all greeted each other, they got down to business.

Jesse's smile turned serious. "I think we have a good lead. Michael flew to Oklahoma City to check it out and will hopefully have answers before the rodeo is over."

"That's where Kramer's outfit's at," Trip said.

"Yes," Sean agreed. "It is. He's going to do some undercover poking around."

"I hope he's careful. I want our horses back but not at the expense of someone getting hurt." A thankfulness swept over Lori as she stood there. Her daddy might not be here but she was surrounded by a tremendous amount of amazing men, counting these three men, the five Presley brothers and their dad, and Trip too. She wasn't sure what she'd done to deserve them but she was thankful. She had the best team a woman could ask for on her side. She felt as if her daddy had been unable to stand by her side so he sent the best he could round up. Lori's heart felt like it would burst. And yet, she also wanted to stand on her own feet and be a part of the solution.

"Michael can take care of himself, so don't worry," Jesse assured her. "We have a man digging around at Kramer's ranch. He's searching the place for any signs of your horses and has a suspicion he might know where they are. We decided one of us needed to be there. He'll be in touch. In the meantime, we're going to hang out here and personally keep our eyes open. This is the WRC and we want this resolved as quickly as possible."

"So do I," she said, glancing at Trip.

"We all want that," Sean said. "Trip tells me that Vance Presley and his brothers are here looking out for your interests too. If we all have our ears open to the conversations and actions around us, something, even something small, might come to light."

"I hope so," she said, just as Sean's phone rang.

"We all do," he said as he unclipped his phone from its clip on his belt. "Excuse me." He moved away from them all as he answered the call.

It didn't last long before he ended it. "I need to head out. There's a lame bull that needs my attention."

"That's fine," Jesse said, then frowned. "Let us know how that turns out. I need to check with the secretary, but I believe Kramer has stock that could benefit from this."

"I don't like the sound of this." Trip frowned.

"I'll let you know what I find out after I look at the animal." Sean slipped out the door, not wasting any more time talking.

Lori was restless. "I think I'll go check on my horses. I'm glad everyone is here, and Daddy would be very appreciative of all the help. I know this may not be all targeted at the Calhoun Ranch and our stock company, but either way it needs to stop. Hopefully, Sean will find that the bull he's looking at is lame for some simple reason. But anyway, call me if any info turns up. And I'll do the same. I'll see y'all later at the rodeo."

"I'll come with you." Trip said goodbye to Jesse and headed out with her.

They left the hotel and walked toward the arena. There were a small group of western-clad singers entertaining people on the steps of the Stock Exchange and the lively music and hustle of tourists made the street a lively place. When she heard the sound of cattle mooing she stared down the street and saw the daily cattle drive coming their way. The reenactment was put on daily for all the tourists at the Stockyards. Lori watched Longhorns and cowboys pass by and again thought of her dad.

She looked at Trip. "I used to love coming here as a girl. I remember the first time I saw them run cattle through here. Daddy picked me up and put me on his shoulders to watch the Longhorns and the cowboys." Those memories seemed etched in her mind more than normal this weekend. It had been a while since she'd come to Fort Worth and the Stockyards. There was so much history in this place, and she and her father's memories were forever etched there for her as deeply as Texas history and the cattle drives of the early days.

"I have memories with my dad too. We loved the

Stockyard Museum and eating at the Cattleman's Steakhouse...that was a treat for a little kid."

"Yes, it was, I'm sure." She shot him an understanding smile. "I hope we have a new memory here that includes finding our horses."

"That would be a fantastic memory for us. I'm just in shock that someone would risk everything to do something like this."

"Me too. But when someone gets himself into financial trouble like he's obviously in, there is no telling what they'll do."

They entered the Coliseum and headed to the stalls. Cooper spotted them and came over. "Hey, glad you're here. There was a guy hanging around earlier. I watched him and he just seemed overly interested in your stock. I finally asked him if he needed any help with anything and he didn't waste any time disappearing. Also, heard through the grapevine that a bull is lame and the owner is furious."

Trip was studying their horses. "Sean Knight is on his way to look at the bull. This guy you saw, what does your gut tell you? Did you think he was up to no good?"

"I do. I kept watching at first to see if he was going to make a move, but no deal. He finally just irritated me and I wanted to see if he'd spook."

"And he did," she said.

"Oh, yes, he did. The question is, why? Like the Knights have stated, this Kramer has a reason for wanting your horses out of the show. But it seems too easy."

"That's what I'm thinking. But then, desperation leads to sloppiness," Trip said. "I think Kramer is a real jerk, but stupid? It's hard for me to believe, and yet it's not looking good for him."

"I'll stick around back here during the rodeo as they take the horses into the chutes."

"Thanks," Lori said as she moved to the fence to study her horses. They all acted like they were in good spirits and that usually meant they were going to put on a good show, which was exactly what she needed from them. With her top five out, these fellas needed to step up and give the bucking performances of their lives.

A few hours later the rodeo was in full swing, and Trip couldn't chase the feeling away that something wasn't right. Maybe he was feeling overly suspicious, but his gut was telling him something was wrong or going to be wrong.

They had men spread out all over the place. Jesse had gone behind the chutes to hang out with the bull riders and they knew that Sean would be around back there too. Especially since the bull that had been lame had been taken out, and one of Kramer's backup bulls had taken its place.

When it was finally time for the saddle bronc competition, Trip could tell Lori was nervous. He reached out and took her hands. "Relax. It's going to be okay. Nothing is going to happen to our horses. We have too many eyes on the ground watching and listening. And Cooper is not going to let anything happen back there. He'll call if we're needed."

"But we need them to figure this out. Not just make it through. When this rodeo ends and we don't have our horses, then we don't make the finals."

He wanted and needed the horses to make the finals. He had something to prove. But seeing the worry on her face, he realized there were more important things than proving he had what it took to keep a business successful.

He pulled her into his arms. "I want to find the horses. I want them safe, and you know I want to compete and show this company is strong. But if we don't meet the deadline, that's just the way it's going to be. We keep going." He kissed her gently with a brief brush of his lips to hers. She stared up at him as if stunned.

"But, what about us?"

He loved the feel of her in his arms. "We're fine. We'll get our situation figured out when everything is settled. But right now, try not to worry. I just want you to realize life doesn't end if we don't have horses in the finals."

She took a deep breath. "Okay, I'll try to relax.

Dad would have said something similar."

"Yes, I believe he would have. Your daddy was a very smart, wise man." He kissed her forehead.

She turned deeply serious. "Yes, he was. He hired you." She placed her arms around his waist and hugged him.

Satisfaction coursed through Trip. "Thank you, that means a lot to me."

"I'm glad we've made it to this point," she said, and the worry in her expression eased. "I'm glad to have you at my side."

"*Up next, Vance Presley*," the announcer called over the loudspeaker. "Riding Dream Wrecker."

They both faced the arena and watched as Vance lowered himself into the chute and settled on the back of the bronc. He hadn't drawn one of theirs, but instead had drawn, of all horses, one of Kramer's. The horse was restless and jumped in the chute, causing Vance to scramble back up on the chute bars with his boots braced on either side of the rowdy saddle bronc. The cowboys holding the bucking horses' reins put pressure on, trying to settle Dream Wrecker down, and after a couple of seconds, Vance yanked on his hat and lowered himself back down.

Trip could see Jesse's head over the stall rungs where he had moved in close and was studying the horse. There was nothing unusual about a restless saddle bronc, though. They were high-strung and ready to rock-n-roll in an event.

In the next moment, the gate opened, and the horse blasted from the chute, bucking and spinning, trying with everything it had to toss Vance to the dirt. Vance rode with all the show and skill of the best, arms back, knees working as he moved with the rhythm of the saddle bronc. One thing about the cowboy, he was one of the best and his trips to the finals were a testament to that. Tonight was no different as he rode Dream Wrecker to the buzzer. The horse was bucking like mad as the pickup men rode in hard to help Vance get off the back of the horse safely. It was always a dangerous moment when the cowboy tried to jump from the bucking horse. The two pickup men came alongside the horse, and one reached for the bucking cinch while the other tried to move in so

Vance could grab his shoulders and swing off Dream Weaver and jump to the ground with the protection of the pickup horse between him and the bronc.

It was not easy when the horse was freaking out as it seemed this one was doing. Finally, Vance managed to throw himself off the horse while holding onto one of the pickup men's shoulders, then slid to the ground unharmed. The good-looking cowboy grinned as his boots hit the dirt. He yanked his hat off his head and fanned it to the roaring crowd as he jogged to the fence.

"Whew," Lori gasped. "Always a showman. I was worried."

"Yeah, that horse was hyped up good."

"Well, they're trying hard for rough stock that will give the guys a tough ride. The tougher the ride, the farther the horse goes."

"True, ours are great in the arena, but that just seemed off to me. Let's go down there. I want to talk to Vance and Jesse."

She heard the skepticism in his voice, and when he started down the bleachers she followed.

CHAPTER TWELVE

They reached the bottom of the stands and headed toward the stock area. Trip wanted to hear what Vance had to say about that horse. And he wanted to hear what Jesse thought too. There had been some drugging of stock a while back and he couldn't help wondering if that had happened again. Kramer was obviously in over his head and desperate. But he didn't want to say anything more to Lori until his suspicions were confirmed. Sean could find out with a simple blood test if the others were suspicious too.

Or maybe he was just being overly touchy where

anything that had to do with Kramer was concerned. Most people watching would only have seen the ride as amazing. They wouldn't have dreamed they were seeing a drugged-up horse that could hurt himself or his rider.

Speak of the devil, Kramer moved from a group of men and slid in front of them, blocking their path. He was a short man with a thick waist and he liked to wear his shirt unbuttoned two buttons too many to expose the gold chain he wore around his neck. But his biggest and worse accessory was his shadow, the six-feet-four cowboy that Trip and many of the others referred to as his *goon*. The man crossed his tree-trunk-sized arms and leveled a glare at them.

"Kramer," Trip acknowledged him. He stepped closer to Lori when he heard her intake of air when she realized who the man was. Trip had forgotten that she still hadn't met the man who was looking more and more like the one who stole their horses.

"Jensen. Miss Calhoun," Kramer drawled in what sounded more like a snarl. "I've been wondering when I was going to run into you. What do you think you're up to?"

Lori shot Trip a questioning look, but he kept his expression stone cold as he returned his gaze to Kramer. It took everything he had to hold his temper in check. "We've been right here. The question is what have you been up to?"

The man blustered. "What does that mean?"

"You asked the question first. We're trying to run a stock business. Trying to figure out who took our horses. You wouldn't happen to know anything about all that, would you?"

He turned red-faced. "Are you accusing me of something?"

Trip cocked his head to the side and stared hard at the bodyguard when he took a step forward. "I'd back up, hoss," he demanded. "We're just having a conversation here that we did not initiate. Kramer either answers my question or steps aside. We're trying to congratulate our good friend on a great ride. Looks like Vance got the better of your bronc."

"I don't believe I've had the pleasure of an introduction, but I'm assuming you are Mr. Kramer and the owner of Vance's ride moments ago?" Lori didn't look at all intimidated.

"That's me," he huffed. "My horse almost got him off. It was still a tough ride and a high score. Presley got lucky."

"You think? I beg to differ." Trip goaded him on purpose. Hoping to see what the man would do. If he had taken their horses, then Trip wanted to push the man and see what happened. All he could hope was that Michael was having good luck on the ground at the man's ranch right now.

"My horses are better than the Calhoun Stock. Your outfit is the one that's had the lucky breaks in the lineup, getting the lesser riders and making your horses look better while mine draw the tougher contenders and it makes them look like a lesser ride. You know it's true." He glared at Lori. "Your daddy always had the luck on his side."

Lori stiffened. "My daddy worked hard and believed in making his own luck happen through his hard work."

Kramer's eyes narrowed. "You're a smart a—"

Trip cut him off. "Watch your mouth, Kramer. Don't start insulting my partner."

The man cut angry eyes at him. "From what I hear, she's your boss. You're just her lackey."

Trip let the cutting words slide off of him, knowing Kramer was just baiting him. "I think we're done here. We have a rider to congratulate. Step aside."

"For now." Kramer moved away and *his* lackey moved with him.

Trip took Lori's arm and moved her past them. He could feel the fight in her in the stiffness of her arm, and could see it in her eyes and the square of her shoulders and jaw. She was brewing for a fight. He tugged harder when she hesitated and glared at Kramer.

"He's my partner. The best there is." Trip pulled hard and forced her to move past Kramer.

"Well, that is just so sweet. She's taking up for you," Kramer snarled sarcastically.

Trip clamped his mouth shut.

"How dare you say something like that," Lori

blurted out. "Who do you think you are, you little twerp—"

Trip grabbed Lori by the arm and hauled her into the crowd and toward the rough stock chutes.

"Why are you pulling on me? I had something to say," she demanded, yanking to get loose from him. But he held on tight.

"Because we'd said enough, and he's not worth wasting any more breath on."

"But what he said isn't true."

"I know that. I'm fine. I crossed that line a while back. Okay? But you didn't need to go pushing any more buttons on the dude than you already had."

"Fine," she snapped. "But he had it coming."

Yeah, that was true. Trip let the words play in his head but said nothing as he tried to ignore the pricks to his pride. Tried to not let the jabs Kramer was trying to hit him with dig in. But deny as he might, deep down the words struck their mark.

Everything about the run-in with Kramer made Lori's

skin crawl. He had intentionally insulted Trip and her dad and tried to go after her, but Trip had stopped him. She wished she'd been able to stop him from insulting Trip. The same ole story always seemed to jump between them. She knew once again she'd had bait tossed at her but Trip had managed to keep her from taking it too far. She had to get better at holding her tongue. But, shoot, the man was a sleazeball.

Vance, Jesse, and Sean were in deep conversation with Marcus Presley when they walked up.

"What's going on?" she asked.

"Something wrong with that ride?" Trip studied them with penetrating eyes that Lori felt all the way to her toes.

"We have our suspicions," Jesse said. "We're not sure if the horse was hyped up to ride harder or what, but Vance did a great job."

Sean did not look happy. "I'm going to test it and see. It might disqualify Vance's ride, but again, substance abuse is easy to detect so if he drugged Dream Wrecker, then he's desperate."

"The deal is," Vance said, "he didn't ride much

different from a regular tough ride. If he's drugged, then it wasn't enough to draw attention to anyone but us. And that's because we're looking for anything that might point a finger at Kramer."

"True," Marcus said. "We could be overly observant. Lori, is something wrong, honey? You looked angry when you walked up here."

"Yes. I just had the unpleasant opportunity to meet Stan Kramer. The man is awful."

Grunts of agreement made the rounds from everyone around her.

"You stay away from him," Trip said. "I got the distinct feeling that this isn't just about rodeo status, but is personal. Your daddy never said a lot about Kramer. He just didn't like him or trust him after that incident with our horse. But when it happened, he also didn't seem surprised. I'm wondering if there is history there we don't know about. Marcus, do you know anything?"

Marcus looked thoughtful, as if searching his memory. If anyone knew anything it would be Marcus, since he and her dad had been best friends since their early years.

"Well, I know your dad always said Stan, or Kramer, as everyone seems to call him nowadays, held grudges for way too long. Said it wasn't healthy."

"But why would he say that?" she asked.

"Yeah," Trip spoke up. "He never said that to me. He just told me to keep a close watch on everything after we suspected him of hurting our horse."

"For one, he used to compete with us in the rodeo and he wasn't as good as us. But it seemed he could never best your dad. I think there was a woman he had a thing for too that wouldn't give him the time of day because she was too busy chasing after your dad. But your dad didn't reciprocate the infatuation and she still wouldn't have anything to do with Kramer. Maybe that's what Ray meant. When it came to talking about women, Ray didn't say much and I didn't either."

"He didn't tolerate any disrespect toward women," Trip said. "I know that for certain. So I can see why he'd keep his mouth closed even when he was being chased by one he didn't want to pursue. So if Kramer has sour apples about that, then the man is putting the blame where it doesn't belong."

"That's for certain," Marcus agreed.

Lori took a deep breath, trying to digest everything. "So do you think all this could be from an old grudge about being rejected by a woman?"

Every man in the group looked at her and shrugged.

"Men have died for lesser reasons all through history," Jesse said. "Right now, that's all we've got, that and his financial problems. He's looking for someone to blame."

She couldn't believe it could be that simple. It was ridiculous. But it was true that people did crazy things.

"Let's call a meeting with everyone over at the stock pens," Trip said. "I'm sure Cooper and Brice are wondering what's going on.

"That'd be great," Drake said, looking as unhappy as she was. "When are the cops going to get involved with this?"

"We're waiting to see what Michael and the local sheriff's department he's working with in Oklahoma can come up with."

"I see," Drake said.

Jesse and Sean led the way out of the crowded chute area and she and Trip followed.

"Are you okay?" he asked.

"I'm mad," she said. "And confused. It just doesn't make sense." She heard someone call her name and turned to see Kelly, a former rodeo friend from college. Her spirits lifted for a moment. "Hey, go on without me. I'll be there as soon as I say hi to an old friend."

He didn't look happy. "I'll stay with you. I don't want you hanging out alone—"

"I'm fine, Trip. I'll be right there. Truth is, I need a break from all this and visiting with Kelly for a moment sounds perfect."

He didn't look happy as Kelly got closer through the throng of people. "Fine. But if you're not back in fifteen minutes, I'll come looking."

She frowned. "Stop worrying. I'll be there when I get through. It won't be long. I'm not going to keep everyone waiting."

"Okay, but call if you need me."

She laughed and shook her head. "Go. I'm fine." As soon as he headed off, she turned and met Kelly in a big hug. Talking to an old friend would help. She was fed up with the craziness going on around her.

CHAPTER THIRTEEN

Trip caught up with Jesse and the Presleys after leaving Lori to visit with her friend. He felt uncomfortable leaving her and was on edge with the way the conversation had gone with Kramer. Something had happened between Kramer and Ray Calhoun. And it was reasonable that someone could hold a grudge for this long. People, as Jess had said, did terrible things for a lot less than being jealous over a woman and being rejected.

Not only had Kramer had a woman reject him because she was crazy about Ray, it was a woman that

Ray hadn't wanted. That would be unsettling for a guy like Kramer. And then Kramer had gone into the rough stock business and so had Ray. And Ray was more successful.

Yeah, Trip got it. He could see where that would grate at a guy. Especially a guy who wasn't dealing with a full deck, it seemed.

But the fact that he hadn't made his whole move until now, after Ray was gone, fit. He was fairly certain that Kramer had poisoned that horse that time and he was sure Ray figured it out. For all Trip knew, since Ray hadn't told a story about that, Ray may have had a meeting of the mind with Kramer about that incident that Trip was not privy to. He could only imagine what a man like Ray said to a man like Kramer. As intimidating as Ray was, with his larger-than-life personality and being so well liked versus the little twerp that Kramer was, Trip could see where Kramer would've probably been shaking in his boots. Until Ray died and his daughter took over. And his financial problems became so terrible and he became desperate. He figured he could pick on Trip and Lori.

He could take their business to ruin and then he would get jobs. When Trip reached the others, and they met up with Cooper and Brice, he relayed what he thought. They all looked unfazed by his assessment.

Marcus was the first to speak up. "I agree with you. I can see where Ray would've probably gone to him, and he wouldn't have tiptoed around the situation. If he thought Kramer had hurt his anima,l Ray would have confronted him. He might not have told you or me because that's the kind of man Ray was. But I guarantee you that behind closed doors, man to man— Ray handled it.

"And that's why his animals didn't get messed with again. But now, like you say, he's desperate, and he's just the kind of man who would pick on a woman—not that you're a woman but you know what I mean. Ray was Lori's daddy, and he's gone and Lori is here. Lori owns the ranch. It's more about her, to be frank."

Trip understood it. He knew Marcus didn't mean any harm by what he said. It was the truth. No matter how hard he worked, no matter how much the success of the rough stock business would and could ultimately be because of his promotion and work, in the end, it would always be that Ray Calhoun's daughter owned the ranch and the business that Ray began. And Trip had just bought into it.

He loved Lori. But could he live with that? The truth of their situation was staring him in the face. But right now, it didn't matter. Right now, it was about getting this business with Kramer settled, getting their horses back, and moving forward.

Jesse's phone rang. He pulled it from its holster. "It's Michael." He stepped away from everybody and they all watched as he listened. His expression was intense. Then furious. The call didn't last long, and he hung up and stalked to them, his expression grave.

"They found the horses. Michael was relentless and his informant worked hard to help him. It was time to go looking while Kramer and his goons weren't around. It took a little while, but they found them in a barn on some property Kramer leases way in the backcountry. They've been neglected all this time. No feed. They're not in good shape but are being looked after now."

Trip spun on his boot heel, fury sweeping through him. He was going for Kramer.

Marcus and Cooper stepped in front of him.

"Hold on," Cooper said.

"Yeah, son," Marcus agreed. "You're in no shape to go after Kramer. Take a deep breath."

"You'd rip his head off." Drake and Brice stepped up to help block him.

"The police are on their way," Jesse told him. "They are probably on the premises as we speak. We need to tell Lori."

The rodeo was ending and people were moving out of the stands. It was a rough time to be trying to find her. Trip suddenly got his senses back. "Yeah, we need to find her. I don't want Kramer getting near her. If he's already been tipped off, then who knows what he'll do if he feels cornered."

Lori was making her way through the rough stock pens when she spotted a group of police officers enter the building at the end of the corridor. One of them stood out in his cowboy hat and starched white shirt with the shining star pinned over his heart. Even at a distance she was pretty sure he was a U.S. Marshal. Her gut told her once more something wasn't right.

She was, of all places, near Kramer's stock pens when she spotted them. And they were coming this way. People were parting the way for them as they came down the corridor. She looked around just as she was grabbed around her neck and yanked hard against a soft body.

"They're not going to pin this on me," the distinctive voice of Kramer growled in her ear.

She yanked harder. "Let me go," she demanded.

"Hold still," he growled.

She was uncertain of what had happened, but obviously something had. "Let me go," she gasped as he tightened his arm around her neck. For a small man, he had surprising strength in his short arms. She tried to kick him in the knee and then grunted. "They're going to stop you."

"Kramer," Trip yelled from the distance. "Let her go. It's over. The police are here. We know what you did with our horses."

"This is the police. Let her go and put your hands up."

Lori heard the anger in Trip's voice and suddenly she wasn't just mad, she was worried. She brought her hands up to grasp the arm wrapped around her neck. She was a little taller than Kramer and he had her yanked hard against him, forcing her to lean back. It was awkward and made his grip on her throat that much more painful. She coughed, which only caused him to hold tighter as he started backing them up.

"Where," she gasped, "are you going? Give up. You're done." She coughed again, her gaze finding Trip in the now-cleared-out corridor. People had scrambled out of there as fast as they could get to safety. Trip stood out in the wide-open, glaring Kramer down. She couldn't find the lawmen in her vision, but they were to the left while Trip and the Presleys and the Knights were to the right. She could see them, her posse standing behind Trip.

She felt the hard bite of a pistol dig into her back.

"I've got a pistol and I'll use it on your girlfriend."

"Don't make this worse on yourself," the lawman called. "Let the lady go and you won't get hurt."

"I'm walking out of here with her," he yelled, loosening his grip on her momentarily.

Lori sucked in a breath. "Why are you doing this?"

"Your daddy ruined me. If it hadn't been for him always getting the luck—"

Lori was dealing with a madman. He had lost all reasoning where her daddy was concerned and blamed everything wrong in his life on him.

"Your bad judgment is what cost you, Kramer. And you're making more bad choices right now. Let Lori go. Do the right thing." Trip was moving cautiously toward them. On the other side, the law had pulled their weapons. Lori suddenly realized someone might not come out of this alive.

Her knees were weak. "Trip, stop," she called.

Fear for him was overwhelming. "Get out of the way."

As if in answer, Kramer pulled his pistol from her ribs and pointed it at Trip.

Trip's heart hammered as he watched the woman he loved being choked and held captive by Kramer. He stared at the gun pointing at him and looked past the madman to see the lawmen fanning out. One was inside the stock pen and moving toward Kramer, using cattle as his shield.

"I'm walking out of here, so move out of the way. All of you. Get in that crosswalk and let me pass or I'll shoot her."

"Don't do that," the U.S. Marshal warned. "Put your weapon down. There's no way out of this."

"Kramer, stop this while you can," Lori urged, feeling the man's desperation and feeling her own as she watched Trip hover between holding back and charging her captor. Fear for him held her in its icy grip. She couldn't bear to lose him. Their eyes locked and panic seized her as she saw his gaze flinch, saw him step forward. "No," she shouted, struggling to stop him from stepping toward the gun leveled at him.

As if in slow motion, she saw him move and felt Kramer panic. His arm jerked, and on instinct she stomped hard on his boot while elbowing him in the gut and twisting hard as the sound of the gun fired...

In that same instant, Kramer's arm loosened and she was free. She stumbled to the ground as two more shots were fired and Kramer fell in the dirt beside her. Her gaze was locked on Trip.

He dropped to his knees as a bloodstain spread across his shoulder, and then he fell face first in the dirt.

CHAPTER FOURTEEN

"Don't you dare leave me, Trip Jensen…"

Trip struggled to roll over. His shoulder hurt like he'd been kicked by a rampaging, two-thousand-pound bucking bull, but all he was focused on was Lori's sweet voice. She was okay.

"I'm not going anywhere," he managed as she helped him onto his back. "I'm staying right here with you, darlin'," he drawled, trying hard not to slur his words, fighting to stay conscious. "You're a beautiful sight."

"Oh, Trip, I thought…" she cried. "I thought I'd lost you."

"Let me in here," Sean Knight said, pushing through the throng of friends hovering over Trip and Lori.

Trip winced when Sean immediately applied hard pressure to his wound.

"It's your shoulder. You'll have a scar, but you'll live. Thanks to Lori fighting like a wildcat to knock that fool's aim off."

Trip gave her a grin. "Seems I owe you my life," he said, wiping the tears from her face with his free hand.

"And I owe you mine," she said through her tears, hearing a smile try to sound in her words. "You shouldn't have done that."

"Done what? Try to save the woman I love?"

She laughed, and her smile sent joy raging through him. "I love you too. But still, thank God and the marshal's good aim we're going to live to enjoy that love."

He felt his head spinning. "Exactly what I was aiming for," he said. And then everything went black.

Two days later

"Okay, open that trailer," Lori instructed. Michael

Knight had warned her that the horses had lost weight but were doing good. Sean had driven to Oklahoma straight from the rodeo after the ambulance had gotten there for Trip. He'd wanted to check them out and monitor their wellbeing, then transport them back to the ranch. He and Michael had gone out of their way to take care of them. Jesse Knight had remained in Fort Worth to help handle any legal issues as all that Stan Kramer had done came to light. She would always be grateful to the Knight Investigation Agency for what they'd done.

But as she glanced around the group waiting along with her and Trip, her heart was full. The handsome Presleys were all gathered around the round pen, including Carson Andrews, their cousin. He strode toward her and hugged her.

"Lori, I'm so sorry this was going on and I couldn't help." He stepped back and grabbed Trip's hand. "I'm glad you're okay."

"Me too," Trip grinned. "And we knew you had your hands full."

Lori felt bad for Carson and the ongoing struggle

he had with his little girl's mother. "You've got your own priorities. Is Julie okay?"

Carson looked troubled but faked a smile. "She's fine, just at that age where she really needs a mom. And her mom…well, she's a little too busy to care."

"She's the loser in all of this. Julie has you and she's a lucky little girl." His wife had run off and left him with a baby to raise and he'd done a good job, but Lori knew he worried that he wasn't good enough and that his little girl missed not having a mother around. He, like all his cousins, was a good, good man, and she hoped one day he'd take a chance on love once more.

"If you need anything while Trip is recovering," Carson said, "please call me. I'll be home now."

"Thanks. Marcus has assured me that if there is anything I need while Trip is recovering, all I need to do is ask and they'll take care of it. So, you all are amazing. I'm sure I'll have all the help I can handle."

"Thanks for the offer," Trip said. "I appreciate the backup."

"I'm here if you need me. You might need to sit down. You look a bit pale still."

"Heading that way with him now," Lori said as Carson headed back to the fence.

She looked at Trip. No one had estimated Trip's determination to be here today. His shoulder had needed extensive surgery, and he'd lost a lot of blood, but he'd gotten his release papers this morning and was standing beside her. His good arm was draped over her shoulders and Lori felt love and security within his shadow. God had been good, and he was still here with her.

Kramer wasn't. He'd died instantly when the U. S. Marshal had fired at him and his bullet hadn't missed. Lori still couldn't believe that he'd blamed all of his bad choices and subsequent bad luck on her daddy. And that he'd felt it was his right to try to ruin what Ray Calhoun had worked so hard to build.

But that was all behind them. Her horses would be ready for the finals. They'd been given a reprieve from the next rodeo, and Sean had said they'd be ready for the next rodeo on the circuit and qualify to participate in the big show, the National Finals in Vegas.

Harvey sat on a horse in the arena, waiting on the

rough stock horses to be released. He had come to her immediately when she arrived home and apologized for acting so negative since losing the horses, and said he'd been defensive when he should have been helpful. He'd also asked if he could help care for the horses so they could be ready for the finals. She'd agreed and felt relief that they could start over, since her daddy had liked Harvey and valued his contribution to the ranch.

"Here they come," Trip said, close to her ear. "Don't be too upset. Remember, Sean said they're doing good."

She nodded as Michael pulled the trailer gate open and the horses ran out of the trailer and into the holding pen. She gasped. "Oh, how could anyone do that to horses?" Her horses were thin from just two weeks without feed; not as bad as some of the wild Mustangs the Presleys and their rescue program took in, but still, they were in a state of neglect. "Thankfully we got to them," she said. "If Kramer wasn't already dead I'd probably be heading to the jailhouse to give him a piece of my mind. How could he?"

"He was a messed-up man. Sometimes nothing explains it."

"Yeah. I guess so." She turned to him. "I'm so glad you're home. You need to sit down."

He smiled and hugged her to him. "I'm fine. We need to talk," he said and then led her away from the arena.

"Hey," Cooper called from where he and Vance were standing with their arms on the arena rungs, studying the horses. "Where are you two lovebirds heading?"

Trip chuckled. "None of your business, Presley. This is between me and my lady."

"Oh, your lady," his friend teased. "Well, y'all go on, then, and I hope you come back in a few minutes and give us some good news."

"Yeah," Vance added with a wink. "Good news. I think it's time for us to have a party around here. If you know what I mean."

Trip laughed and Lori shook her head and chuckled. "I kind of like the idea of a party, too," she said, and then hugged him tight as they walked into the barn.

Trip stopped outside his office and turned to pull her close with his good arm. "I love you, Lori. And I've struggled with objection after objection as to why I can't ask you to be my wife. I don't have what you have and I might not ever have enough to equal what you have. That rankles on a man, but, your ranch aside, I can build something with you with the rough stock business that we can share together. I like that. But most of all I like the idea of building a life with you. I'm tired of putting it off. Of not telling you how much I love you. It's eating away at me, and the other night when Kramer had you all I could think about was all the time we'd wasted. I don't want to spend another hour without you in my life. I can take anything but that. Will you marry me?"

Her arms were already around his waist, but they tightened and her eyes were bright with tears. "I have waited so long to hear you say that. Yes, yes, and yes. I love you and want to start our lives together. Now, as soon as possible." She carefully leaned into him, and he kissed her as the sunbeam from the entrance of the barn spotlighted them and the warmth of her love spread through him.

"Then I do believe we're ready for that party."

She touched his face with tender fingers. "Trip, I've waited my whole life for this party. It's going to be amazing."

"You're amazing," he said, and then he settled his lips on hers and kissed her with all the love in his heart…

It was a long time before they left the barn to share their news.

Excerpt from

THE COWBOY'S BRIDE FOR HIRE

Cowboys of Ransom Creek, Book Two

CHAPTER ONE

"**Y**ou need a wife."

"Those are fighting words." Carson Andrews shot his cousin a scowl. "Had the one and never another, and you know it. Why would you even say that?"

"For one thing, it's been two years, Carson. It may be time to move on." Cooper Presley hitched a brow and shoved a newspaper at Carson. "But if that's not cool, then you need a wife for a day. Just a day, that's all I'm saying. Read that ad and you'll understand."

Baffled, Carson stared down at the newspaper.

Single males in need of a bride for a day? This is strictly an at-your-service business proposition. Absolutely no romance involved. Do you need the eyes of a woman to help plan and/or set up an event or decorate a space with your personal interest and taste in mind, but with an added touch of your bride—if you had one? Then call Bride for Hire and let me do the work...

"That right there is a bona fide perfect solution for your situation." Cooper grinned at him. "A little unconventional, but still, you need a woman's touch. And she's just in Fort Worth, so that's not so far away that she couldn't come out here to help you out. It's worth a call at least."

Carson looked around the kitchen. It was about as featureless as a hospital room: Nothing on the walls.

The counter held a coffee pot and a can of coffee beside it. And the living room beyond the bar area was just as plain. He thought of April's room and frowned. It wasn't much better with the only decorations being a floor full of scattered toys and a bed. At least the bed did have a colorful comforter.

A knot formed in Carson's gut. "You're right. As much as I hate to admit it, I could use someone to help get this place into shape. With April turning five at the end of the month, I guess I need to start learning how to decorate and bake cookies and give her what she is missing."

Cooper laughed. "They do make those kind you buy at the grocery store and just cut up and then bake. I don't think the situation is so bad that you have to break out the flour and start burning down the house."

"Hey, I could do it if I set my mind to it. And who says you could do any better? Last I counted, you and your four brothers were all still single and cared more about your horses than decorating."

Cooper squinted in the sunshine. "That'd be an accurate account for certain, but we don't have a little girl who needs to be wearing tutus and having tea parties and such."

Carson shot his cousin an exasperated glare. "I've been having tea parties for over two years now, so don't even go there."

"Well, that's just great, but you're falling down in other areas."

His mind churning, Carson led the way across the wide expanse of yard to the barn. There was a round pen off the back where a huge black bull waited. Carson was putting him in the sale in two weeks at Cooper's family ranch in Ransom Creek and Cooper was here to see him.

Cooper stopped at the fence and squinted at Carson. "Why haven't you asked one of the women around here in Bride to help you out?"

"Not a good idea. I'm not interested in starting anything up with anyone from Bride. I know there are a few ladies in town who'd welcome the thought of coming out here and helping me. They have made that clear. And they're nice ladies, for the most part, although there are a few I avoid at all cost. I don't want to mislead anyone into thinking I'm going to need a woman hanging around for a future with me. There is no future with me. I've been through the wedding fiasco and it won't happen again."

Cooper looked skeptical. "It's not like you got jilted like that bride this town put that statue up for. Choosing one bad bride is no reason not to start thinking it would happen again."

"I'm not getting married again, Coop. Ever. I'm going to raise April, put up with her mother when she shows up for visits—if she shows up—and that's all I'm ready for at this point."

"But it's been two years. You aren't even dating again, are you?"

"Nope. I am not," Carson said.

Cooper stared at him as if he'd lost his mind. "Okay, I get it. She tore you up, I know that. But, man, you have got to move on."

"I'm going to call that number after you leave. I like the part on the ad that said *absolutely* no romance involved. I don't know what made her put such strong wording like that in her ad, but as far as I'm concerned it is her main selling point."

"Fine," Cooper grumbled. "Whatever it takes, just as long as you call. April will thank you."

Carson didn't want his daughter to thank him, he just wanted to do the right thing for her. She was his only reason for doing this. If it were up to him, the house was just fine the way it was. Since his ex-wife had run off a little over two years ago, he hadn't had much appetite for decorations. He'd walked out of the house he'd shared with Missy and barely took his clothes and a few sticks of furniture. He'd tried hard to wipe the slate clean of everything about Missy other than his baby girl. The thing was, he knew most of that came from a sense of betrayal he felt—and anger. He knew good and well it was time to start trying to let some of that go. No matter what Missy had done to him, she was the mother of his sweet, growing girl and he had to try to deal with her in a way that would help April have as normal a life as possible. He was thankful every day that he had custody of April. But sad for April that Missy hadn't even wanted it.

He pushed it all to the back of his thoughts as he

led the way to the bull. It was time to talk business. And in two hours, it would be time to pick April up from the babysitter. The fact she was turning five was craziness to him. She was growing up at the speed of light.

And she was the light of his world.

He'd make the call. It was time to make sure she had everything she needed to flourish. At least everything in his power to give her and hope that made up for the things he couldn't give her.

Bella Reese slowed as she saw the entrance to Carson Andrews ranch on the outskirts of Bride, Texas. It hadn't been a bad drive, only two hours because her condo was on the outskirts of Fort Worth and not in the heart of the city or on the far side. When she'd received the call from the divorced father three days ago, she'd been intrigued by his request.

Since opening her new business six months earlier, she'd been moderately busy. Which was a blessing. But instead of helping decorate homes for clients, creating a warm and happy environment like she'd dreamed she would be doing, she'd been hosting business events. They paid the bills, but so far had not satisfied the deep-rooted desire to help someone actually warm up their home. Carson Andrews's call had sent a shaft of joy ringing through her when he'd explained in not so many words that his little girl was turning five soon and he wanted to turn his house into a home, and do whatever she thought to make it a great place for his growing daughter. And he thought while she was at it, maybe she could help him with the birthday party plans.

Oh joy, oh joy! Bella had agreed to the job, and after ending the call, she'd literally danced around her condo she was so excited. She was going to make this the best home Mr. Andrews and April had ever seen. For that privilege and the price he was paying her, the two-hour drive back and forth was well worth it. Truth be told, she would have taken the job for less, just to have the satisfaction of doing what she longed to do. It would also help her portfolio, but that was less important to her than the satisfaction element.

She really needed the feeling of fulfillment that something like this could give her.

She needed it more than anyone close to her understood or knew.

It was a short drive up the red dirt road. The barn came into view first, and off to the side was the house. But it was the man riding the horse in the round pen next to the barn who had her attention. He sat straight in his saddle and had the horse backing up and then turning several quick circles, stirring up dirt as the cowboy expertly road out the quick spin. The two moved as one and she almost ran off the drive watching man and horse. Her tires hit a bump, and she realized too late that she'd been distracted and drove her car into the corner post of the fence.

She yanked the wheel and slammed on the brake. But it wasn't in time to save the fence or the front fender of her car.

She gasped. Her heart thundered as she stared out the window at what she'd done.

This was not the way to make a good first impression.

Carson saw the car just as it scraped its front fender along the corner post of his entrance fence, knocking it slightly crooked while doing far more damage to the small cranberry-toned sedan. He'd set that post himself and knew it wasn't budging much. The metal fender, on the other hand, did not fare as well.

Dismounting, he led the colt over and tied it to the post. Then he opened the gate and strode across the gravel toward the accident. His first thought was that something had happened to the driver to cause him or her to hit the post. After all, how could you not see the thick post that was nearly the size of a telephone pole?

The door opened before he reached the car. A woman climbed out and stared at the car, her hands on slim hips. She spun toward him as he reached her.

"I am so sorry," she gasped, waving a hand toward the fence. "I cannot believe I did this."

He halted beside the post as the woman's alarmed

apple-green eyes slammed into him. "I can't believe you did it either," he said, because it was the truth. "What happened? But more important, are you okay?"

She was pretty, with thick, dark hair and a gentle look to her features that gave the first impression of a gentle soul...but then again, he knew very well that looks could be deceiving.

"I'm fine. Just fine." Her mouth dropped open again as she stared at the leaning post. "I am so very sorry. I was watching you...I mean, I was driving up the drive and I glanced over and saw you and the horse spinning and I, well, I..." She halted and turned practically fire-engine red. "I mean, I forgot to look at the road and took out your pole."

He laughed. He couldn't help it. "Haven't you ever seen a cowboy on a horse before?"

"Yes. I just got caught up in how smooth the maneuver looked. It was beautiful. It really was. But still, I did this." She looked from him to the pole, then to the car, and she cringed.

"I can tell you that the pole will live. I feel worse for your car." He was also glad April was at the babysitter's.

"Your daughter—I could have hit your daughter," she gasped again, looking not just alarmed but horrified. Her hand went to her mouth. "I can't even think about that. I am not normally so careless. I'll pay for damages and promise you it won't happen again. I am so sorry."

Carson appreciated her concern. He had been expecting Bella Reese and he decided this must be her. "Look, April's fine. She's at the babysitter's. Let's not go that direction with what could have happened. I don't take you as being the careless type, so it's all fine. You must be Bella Reese."

She took a deep breath and nodded. Then she held out her hand. "I'm Bella, and this isn't normally my way of making a good first impression."

He smiled. "You've made an entrance, that's for certain. But you've made a good impression in some ways. You cared. Just the alarm on your face shows me that. So it's fine. Knock down another post and then my impression of you will shift." He enjoyed watching the expression on her face relax. He took her hand; his pulse bolted into overdrive as he felt her fingers wrapped around his. Her beautiful eyes collided into his and he saw her awareness in the emerald depths. He released her hand like it was a sizzling pan.

She pulled hers back at nearly the same instant and he had to fight not to take a step away from her. As if that would stop the sudden and powerful awareness of Bella Reese as a woman.

How long had it been since that feeling had hit him? He wasn't going there and slammed the door on that thought.

He rammed his hands on his hips and stared at her fender for a moment. "I'm not sure you'll be able to drive back to Fort Worth. We better make sure it didn't mess up anything with the impact."

"Okay, but I'm so sorry, this was not in the plan. I'm here to do a job for you. Not cause you problems in the middle of your workday."

"It'll be fine." He moved past her and squeezed into the driver's seat of the small car. He felt like a sardine in a matchbox. *How did women drive these cars?* "Stand back and I'll move it into the yard and make sure it's handling right."

"Sure, thank you."

He looked up at her and saw a hint of a smile at the corners of her mouth.

"You laughing at my situation? This car size should be outlawed."

She seemed to relax as a hesitant smile bloomed. "I'm not meaning to laugh at your expense, but you are a car full."

"To put it mildly," he drawled, suddenly not thinking about his situation. He could barely pull his gaze off the way she looked, standing there and looking down at him. She was gorgeous—and he needed to be thinking that like he needed a swift kick in the gut by his horse. "Move back," he snapped, and yanked his thoughts back to where they needed to be.

She immediately stepped back.

He slammed the door and moved the car forward. "What is wrong with you," he muttered as he drove the car to the house. Something scraped against the tire and he stopped. The fender would have to be worked on before she could drive the car. He took a moment inside the car to get his head together. Bella Reese was pretty, seemed nice and sincere. She was here to do a job and the fact that he was reacting to her like a cowpoke on his first date was ridiculous. He scowled as he pushed open the door and managed to get himself to a standing position without having to crawl out of the car and then stand up.

She had followed him and stood waiting for him to regain his upright posture.

He saw the twinkle in her eyes and reminded himself again that he wasn't interested. He straightened his hat. "You're going to need that fender pulled out. It's rubbing against your tire and will probably give you a blowout."

Her forehead crinkled above thoughtful eyes. "So, I'll need a body shop. Or a wrecker service. I'll have to get an estimate for my insurance. Probably rent a car. Does Bride have a rental car place?"

"No car rental, but Bud can fix it and he can tow you if it needs to be towed. He's good."

"Okay, if you'll excuse me, I'll call the insurance and get this settled and then we can talk about the job you've hired me to do. I truly apologize for all of this."

He cocked his head. "Relax, I'm fine. I'll go unsaddle my horse while you make your calls and I'll meet you on the deck. You're welcome to talk up there if you want."

"Thanks, Mr. Andrews."

"Carson. I'm not much on formality."

"Carson, then," she said and headed toward the house.

He strode back across the stretch of grass and gravel to the round pen. This scenario was already looking like more than he bargained for. Then again, she hadn't meant to nearly take down the fence or crunch her car. And he was suddenly wondering whether she seemed to have the same effect on all her clients that she'd had on him. Maybe there was a real strong reason she'd put that disclaimer in her ad. One thing was certain: he would get himself back on track and sternly remind himself that this was a strictly business proposition, just like her ad said.

He reminded himself as he unbuckled the saddle and pulled it off his horse that he wasn't interested anyway.

Not now, not ever again.

More Books by Debra Clopton

Sunset Bay Romance
Longing for Forever (Book 1)
Longing for a Hero (Book 2)
Longing for Love (Book 3)

Texas Brides & Bachelors
Heart of a Cowboy (Book 1)
Trust of a Cowboy (Book 2)
True Love of a Cowboy (Book 3)

New Horizon Ranch Series
Her Texas Cowboy (Book 1)
Rafe (Book 2)
Chase (Book 3)
Ty (Book 4)
Dalton (Book 5)
Treb (Book 6)
Maddie's Secret Baby (Book 7)
Austin (Book 8)

Cowboys of Ransom Creek
Her Cowboy Hero (Book 1)
The Cowboy's Bride for Hire (Book 2)
Cooper: Charmed by the Cowboy (Book 3)
Shane: The Cowboy's Junk-Store Princess (Book 4)
Vance: Her Second-Chance Cowboy (Book 5)
Drake: The Cowboy and Maisy Love (Book 6)
Brice: Not Quite Looking for a Family (Book 7)

Turner Creek Ranch Series
Treasure Me, Cowboy (Book 1)
Rescue Me, Cowboy (Book 2)
Complete Me, Cowboy (Book 3)
Sweet Talk Me, Cowboy (Book 4)

Texas Matchmaker Series
Dream With Me, Cowboy (Book 1)
Be My Love, Cowboy (Book 2)
This Heart's Yours, Cowboy (Book 3)
Hold Me, Cowboy (Book 4)
Be Mine, Cowboy (Book 5)
Marry Me, Cowboy (Book 6)
Cherish Me, Cowboy (Book 7)
Surprise Me, Cowboy (Book 8)
Serenade Me, Cowboy (Book 9)
Return To Me, Cowboy (Book 10)
Love Me, Cowboy (Book 11)
Ride With Me, Cowboy (Book 12)
Dance With Me, Cowboy (Book 13)

Windswept Bay Series
From This Moment On (Book 1)
Somewhere With You (Book 2)
With This Kiss (Book 3)
Forever and For Always (Book 4)
Holding Out For Love (Book 5)
With This Ring (Book 6)
With This Promise (Book 7)
With This Pledge (Book 8)
With This Wish (Book 9)
With This Forever (Book 10)
With This Vow (Book 11)

About the Author

Bestselling author Debra Clopton has sold over 2.5 million books. Her book OPERATION: MARRIED BY CHRISTMAS has been optioned for an ABC Family Movie. Debra is known for her contemporary, western romances, Texas cowboys and feisty heroines. Sweet romance and humor are always intertwined to make readers smile. A sixth generation Texan she lives with her husband on a ranch deep in the heart of Texas. She loves being contacted by readers.

Visit Debra's website at www.debraclopton.com

Sign up for Debra's newsletter at
www.debraclopton.com/contest/

Check out her Facebook at
www.facebook.com/debra.clopton.5

Follow her on Twitter at @debraclopton

Contact her at debraclopton@ymail.com

If you enjoyed reading *Her Cowboy Hero* I would appreciate it if you would help others enjoy this book, too.

Recommend it. Please help other readers find this book by recommending it to friends, reader's groups and discussion boards.

Review it. Please tell other readers why you liked this book by reviewing it on the retail site you purchased it from or Goodreads. If you do write a review, please send an email to debraclopton@ymail.com so I can thank you with a personal email. Or visit me at: www.debraclopton.com.

Made in the USA
Columbia, SC
14 June 2021